you go, he said

"Why else would I spend the whole morning looking for you?"

Gemma stopped and stared at Paul Verignac, wide-eyed. "But why? If you've changed your mind about the damages to your car, I'm still willing to pay for them."

He looked annoyed. "Do you really think I'd go chasing all over Zermatt to get money from you? You don't know me very well, *mademoiselle*."

"I don't know you at all and I don't want to," Gemma retorted angrily. "Will you please leave me alone?"

Paul sighed exasperatedly. "You are one of the most beautiful women I've ever met, and the most argumentative. Or is it only with me that the sparks start to fly?"

His hand gently traced the outline of her mouth. Gemma's heart began to beat painfully....

The Ice Maiden

by

SALLY WENTWORTH

Harlequin Books

TORONTO·LONDON·NEW YORK·AMSTERDAM
SYDNEY·HAMBURG·PARIS·STOCKHOLM

Original hardcover edition published in 1979
by Mills & Boon Limited

ISBN 0-373-02310-3

Harlequin edition published January 1980

Printed in U.S.A.

CHAPTER ONE

'NONSENSE! Within ten years every aspect of life will be run by computers. There isn't a trade or service that can't be run more efficiently when it's programmed by them.'

Gemma Kenyon smiled to herself as she looked round at her apartment mates who were all, as usual, getting tensely involved in the topic under discussion. It had become a ritual between the four of them as they curled up in armchairs or sat on the floor with their mugs of cocoa, grouped round the glowing embers of the fire, the curtains pulled close to shut out the chill winds of the winter evening. Their arguments, although heated at the time, always ended amicably enough; they had known each other too long to let any verbal disagreements intrude on their friendship. Ever since they had first arrived at Oxford as green students they had been drawn together by mutual interests and outlook. As soon as they could they found an apartment in a big old Victorian house on the outskirts of the town and moved in together, much preferring the privacy and freedom this gave them after the restrictions of living-in at their college.

It was usually Angie Mead who started the discussions, as she had tonight. Of the four of them she was probably the most brilliant, although their combined brain-power, with two B.A.s and two B.Sc.s between them, was formidable. A tall girl with fair hair cropped very short and large-lensed glasses, Angie was arguing now that computers could be used in any situation.

'I don't agree,' Gemma broke in. 'There are certain

situations where a computer would be absolutely useless. Anything that has to do with human emotions, for example. How could a glorified calculator possibly be programmed to show compassion, or take likes and dislikes into account?'

Angie glowered at this disparaging description of her beloved computers as Gemma had known she would, and immediately rose to the bait. 'Huh! It's obvious you're not a scientist. Have you never heard of computer dating? You just feed people's preferences into it.'

'Yes, but that's rather hit or miss,' Joy Shepherd, a petite redhead, put in. 'You can get two people who in theory would be perfectly compatible, but who take one look at each other and hate one another on sight. There has to be some basic chemistry as well as mutual interests.'

'I'm sure that those fail mostly because there isn't enough information or because the people give untrue facts about themselves; they fill in the questionnaires as the type of person they'd like to be, not as they really are. I mean, who's going to fill in a form saying they're fat, lazy and bald?'

They all laughed as Lisa Burnett, the fourth member of the quartet, joined in the debate. She had a great sense of humour and could be guaranteed to get the argument back on an even keel if it threatened to get out of hand.

'I still think that brain-power, which is what computers are basically, can be used in that sort of situation,' Angie pursued. 'We've been doing some experiments along these lines recently and I believe you can even use a computer to get yourself a husband—any man you want.'

'Oh, come on, that's impossible,' Gemma said incredulously.

'A sort of scientific love potion,' Lisa laughed.

Angie glared at them as they deliberately provoked her into getting even more determined to convince them. 'No, it isn't impossible. Suppose you decided you wanted to marry someone—anyone—a television star, for example. Call him Mr X. I believe that if you went about it scientifically, exactly following the instructions of the computer; you could be married to him within three months.'

'Even if you'd never met him before?'

'Yes. Even if you'd never met him.'

They were all staring at her now in genuine amazement, and Angie went on quickly before they could start arguing. 'All you have to do is to find out as much as possible about Mr X and feed it into the computer, the print-out will tell you exactly what type of woman he prefers: looks, interests, everything. Then you mould yourself into the same type of woman, and bingo! He's hooked!'

'What makes you so sure he'd fall for the same type?' Gemma asked, fascinated despite herself. 'He might go for a different kind of woman every time.'

'Well, then you'd just have to make yourself like someone he hasn't tried yet. But it's a well known fact that men go for the same kind of woman over and over again; they have very little imagination,' Angie added disparagingly.

Gemma grinned; Angie was the most forceful Women's Libber among them, although they had all found that they could get along very well without men, thank you very much. There had been lapses, of course, during the four years they had been up at Oxford; it was almost inevitable when you had four good-looking girls in a town where the male students greatly outnumbered the female. Each of them had succumbed to some extent to the obdurate advances of some predatory male at one time or another, but they had come to their senses in time and had escaped the ties of a going-steady twosome or the more permanent relationships of living together or marriage.

'What makes you so sure it would work?' Joy was asking. 'Have you actually tried it?'

'Well, no, not this particular experiment, but the statistics prove that. . . .'

'Oh, statistics, is that all? You can bend those any way you like, make them say whatever you want them to say,' Joy said disparagingly.

Goaded, Angie retorted angrily, 'All right, I bet you anything you like it would work. Just give me a chance to prove my theory, that's all I ask.'

'How much are you willing to bet?' Lisa asked teasingly, still not taking her seriously.

Angie thought for a moment, then, 'If I lose I'll take you all out to dinner at the best restaurant in town. How about that?'

The others looked at her in surprise.

'I think she really means it,' Gemma exclaimed incredulously. 'But, Angie, how on earth do you go about proving a thing like that?'

'It's really quite simple. All we have to do is pick a man and feed his details into the computer, then we'll find which one of us suits him best and proceed from there. The computer will tell us how to go about it.'

'One of *us*!' They were all staring at her now.

'Well, of course one of us. Between us we represent more or less every height and colouring, and none of us is exactly ugly. Besides, it will be much easier to carry out the experiment if we keep it between ourselves. I might even use it as part of my thesis for my post-graduate degree,' she added, getting more enthusiastic by the minute.

'But we none of us want to get married, especially to

some pop star or actor. We all swore never to get married at all, remember?' Joy reminded her.

'Well, it needn't go as far as that. We just want Mr X to propose—you don't have to accept the proposal.'

Gemma, seeing that Angie was getting carried away, decided to call a halt. 'It's a nice idea, but completely impractical, of course.' She yawned and rose. 'I'm tired and I've got an early appointment with my tutor tomorrow.'

But Lisa pulled her back into her chair. 'No, don't go, this is getting interesting. Which man would you choose?' she asked Angie.

'Anyone you like, as long as he isn't already married.'

'But famous people move in exalted circles. You'd probably never be able to get near enough to even meet him,' Joy objected.

'On the contrary; it's just because Mr X would be famous that you *could* get near him. You can always find out where they're appearing or what clubs and restaurants they frequent. Then you go there until they notice you.'

'That's crazy,' Gemma broke in. 'How on earth do you expect us to go and hang around some nightclub? We have neither the time nor the money, for a start.'

'We do have time. We have the whole of the Christmas vacation coming up in just a few weeks,' Angie retorted.

'And I'm willing to finance the experiment,' Lisa broke in. 'It sounds fun.'

Lisa was the only rich one among them, her father owning large industrial interests and providing her with a more than generous allowance.

'But we can't do it,' Gemma persisted. 'It's morally wrong.'

'Rubbish!' Angie said dismissively. 'It's purely a scientific experiment. Now, who shall we choose?'

'How about Prince Charles, he's an eligible bachelor?' Joy suggested, tongue in cheek.

'He's a bit too exalted,' Angie laughed, her face flushed with eagerness. 'We want someone slightly more available.' She picked up some glossy magazines and began to flick through them. 'There's that new pop group who are number one on the hit parade,' she suggested, showing them a photograph.

Gemma went rather reluctantly to join the others as they knelt on the floor round Angie.

'They've all got pink hair!' Joy exclaimed. 'No way am I going to hang around for someone with pink hair.'

'How about this actor?' Lisa ventured. 'He's just landed a lead role in a West End play.'

'No, he's no good. I read that he's engaged to the star of that new Emmanuelle film,' Joy answered.

They leafed through several magazines without finding anyone suitable and Gemma was beginning to hope that they would abandon the idea, when Angie exclaimed triumphantly, 'I've found someone! Look, he'd be perfect.'

She held out an old Sunday paper colour supplement and the others crowded round to look. There was a moment's silence and then Joy said in reverential tones, 'He's gorgeous! Who is he?'

'Here, let me see.' Gemma took the magazine from Angie and looked at the photograph. It was taken somewhere in the West Indies, with palm trees edging a long white beach and with a beautiful yacht moored in the background. And in the foreground there was a man dressed only in a pair of casual bathing shorts, his tall, muscular body smooth and tanned. But it was his face that immediately arrested her attention, for it was almost classically handsome, with clean-cut lines and lean cheeks, the softness of his rather long lashes belied by the strength of his firm chin, and only a rather cynical look in his dark eyes and a slight, ironic quirk to his mouth detracting from the handsomeness of his features beneath thick rather long, dark hair. He was a very attractive man, if one liked that sardonic, mocking type.

'His name is Paul Christian Verignac,' Angie was saying. 'You must have heard of him; he's *the* latest international playboy. What does the article say about him?' She took the magazine back. 'He's thirty-two, French, single and fabulously wealthy with estates in the South of France and Normandy, a house in Paris, a villa in Monte Carlo, etc., etc. Likes all sports, especially skiing and sailing, and has had affairs with a whole lot of beautiful women ever since he inherited his father's fortune. He couldn't be better for Mr X,' she enthused. 'We'll be able to find out all about him easily. He's perfect!'

'Now wait a minute,' Gemma said determinedly. 'This has gone far enough. You're letting the whole thing get out of hand. You can't possibly conduct this kind of experiment; you're playing with people's lives and emotions. It isn't fair to....'

'Oh, Gemma, don't be such an old fuddy-duddy. Whose emotions are we playing with? Not ours, because to us this is just a cold-blooded experiment, and certainly not with this Paul Verignac's; one woman more or less definitely isn't going to make any difference to the list he's got already. So where's the harm?' Before Gemma could answer she held up her hand. 'But okay, if you object we'll do this democratically. All those in favour of conducting this experiment?' She raised her hand as did Joy and Lisa. 'Three against one. All those in favour of making Monsieur Paul Verignac the subject of the experiment?'

The others again raised their hands while Gemma sat silently, a slight frown between her brows.

Angie grinned. 'Then that's settled. Now all I have to do is find out everything I possibly can about our chosen subject and feed it into the computer. Then we'll decide which one of us will be most suitable to carry out the experiment. Come on, Gemma, don't look like that. You were outvoted, you know, and we agreed right from the beginning that this flat is always to be run on democratic principles.'

Shrugging resignedly, Gemma said, 'It seems I have no choice. Okay, count me in.'

It took Angie three weeks of hard work before she had collected all the material she could find on Paul Verignac and fed it into the computer at the university. As before, they were all grouped round the fire in their sitting-room, only now it was well into December and there was a sharp frost in the air that made them build up the fire into a bright flame. Lisa bent over it, toasting crumpets on the end of a long toasting fork, while Joy was responsible for spreading the butter and passing them round.

Angie took a wad of computer print-out sheets from her briefcase and started to give them a summary of the results. 'As I expected, it was quite easy to find out about our subject, Paul Verignac,' she began in a businesslike tone. 'Not only had the gossip columnists all over Europe written him up on every possible occasion, but he has also given three in-depth interviews over the past five years, two for French magazines and one for an American paper, so I was able to get a great deal of information about him. But I felt that for the nature of this experiment we needed more intimate details regarding his likes and dislikes in women.' She paused for dramatic effect. 'So I pretended to be a journalist doing a story and went to London to interview two women with whom he's been known to have affairs.' She gave a gratified grin as she saw the surprised looks on the other's faces.

'What did they tell you?' Lisa asked in eager curiosity. 'I bet it was juicy!'

'I'll say!' Angie forgot her businesslike role for a moment as she became purely female. 'According to them he's really something—in bed and out of it. Both of the girls said that he treated them as if they were the only women in the world, that he has a devastating charm and he's a fantastic lover. He swept them off their feet and all that.'

'I'll bet,' Gemma said cynically. 'They probably only said that as a sap to their own consciences. If he was so marvellous, how come they split up with him?'

'Well, they tried to make out that it was the opposite, of course, but it turned out that he dropped them, either because he'd found someone new or because he'd tired of them.'

'Playboy is right! He sounds like a creep to me,' Gemma remarked caustically.

'What did they look like?' Joy asked in some anticipation.

'I think it would be best if I gave you the computer results for that,' Angie suggested, reverting to her former manner. 'As I said, we fed in everything we knew about Mr X and came up with the following.' She cleared her throat. 'His ideal woman would be in the age range twenty to twenty-eight—he doesn't go for older women. She must be interested in sport to the extent of being able to participate with him, especially in sailing and skiing, but she mustn't be sports mad, if you see what I mean. He likes his women to be well-dressed and soignée, doesn't go for jeans and sweater types at all.'

They looked round at each other and giggled; they were dressed to a woman in faded jeans and thick sweaters.

Ignoring this, Angie went on, 'As for intelligence, he doesn't seem too fussy, although he definitely doesn't

go for the really brainy type—one girl tried to improve
his mind and he dropped her like the proverbial hot
potato. So whichever one of us is picked will have to
play down that side of it. Now let me see—oh, yes, he
particularly likes an aura of mystery,' she added as she
turned a sheet of the print-out. 'From interviewing
those two women I gathered that it was because he got
to know them too well that he eventually dropped
them, so we would have to be sure to maintain some
element of mystery. As for wealth and position; he
doesn't seem to mind too much,' she went on. 'Obviously in the jet-set circles he moves in, he's more likely
to meet well-to-do girls, but he's also dated model girls,
film starlets, and a few other career girls, so he's not too
fussy on that score.'

'Anyone who comes along, in fact,' Gemma put in
drily.

'He might have dated all those girls, but he might be
more particular when he's choosing a wife, and that is
what this experiment is aimed at, isn't it—marriage?'
Lisa asked.

'That's true,' Angie agreed. 'I'll make a note to feed
that query into the computer.'

'Come on, Angie,' Joy said impatiently. 'You still
haven't told us what his ideal woman looks like. We
want to know which one of us is going to take part in
the experiment.'

'You sound as if you'd be quite willing to take it on
yourself,' Gemma remarked as she licked some drips
of butter from a crumpet off her fingers.

'Well, I wouldn't mind,' Joy admitted with a rather
sheepish grin. She looked up at the colour supplement
picture that they'd pinned on the wall. 'He really is
dishy,' she sighed.

'Come on, Angie, put her out of her misery. Tell us
who it's to be,' Lisa commanded.

But Angie refused to be hurried. 'I fed the statistics of every woman I could discover that he'd been out with over the last five years into the computer—I thought that was a reasonable length of time because his taste has probably matured during that period. Agreed?'

They all nodded dutifully, and Joy said impatiently, 'Will you please get on with it.'

'Okay, okay. The ideal measurements came out at thirty-four, twenty-four, thirty-six. So as we're all near enough that size there's no problem there. But the next bit thins us out a little. Mr X is tall himself; six feet, one and a half inches, to be precise, and he always goes for tall girls; he's never been known to go for anyone under five feet five.'

Joy and Lisa looked at one another and Joy's face was definitely crestfallen. 'Nobody seems to realise that good things come in small packages any more,' she said wistfully, making the other three laugh at her downcast air.

Both she and Lisa were on the short side, so that left only Gemma and Angie who were over the required height.

'Perhaps it's about time he had a change,' Gemma suggested blandly.

'This is going to be a scientifically controlled experiment,' Angie reminded her tartly. 'We have to follow the computer's instructions exactly or the whole thing is a waste of time. And the computer says the girl has to be over five feet five,' she added firmly.

Rebuffed, they sat silent while she glared at them. Then, satisfied, she went on, 'I also found that apart from tall, willowy girls, he prefers them to have long blonde hair.'

Gemma laughed. 'You've picked yourself out, then. You're the only one with blonde hair.'

'I said *long* blonde hair,' Angie reminded them. 'Mine is short and there isn't time to grow it long.'

'You could wear a wig,' Joy suggested.

'If I could, so could Gemma.'

'That's true. Or else Gemma could dye her hair blonde.'

They all looked at her and Gemma flushed. 'I am *not* going to dye my hair,' she said forcefully.

'It would be a shame,' Lisa agreed. 'That dark chestnut hair is perfect for your colouring, especially with tawny brown eyes like yours.'

'When you've quite finished discussing Gemma's looks, perhaps you'd like me to go on describing Mr X's ideal woman,' Angie broke in sarcastically.

They gave her their attention again and she went on, 'Right, so far we know he likes tall blondes. The computer also tells us that he prefers women who are tanned, who can speak French—although they don't have to be French—who don't wear glasses, and they should preferably have blue eyes.'

'Well, that lets us all out, then,' Gemma said quickly. 'None of us have got blue eyes.'

'No,' Angie agreed dispiritedly, 'I'm afraid that's true. And it's such a shame, because that's the only problem we can't overcome. But to conduct the experiment correctly we would have to do exactly as the computer recommends. It would be cheating if we had someone with different colour eyes.'

'Not necessarily,' Lisa broke in. 'When I spent that summer vacation working with a drama company I learned quite a lot about stage make-up and that sort of thing, and I found that actors quite often use contact lenses to change the colour of their eyes. It's not much different from wearing a wig really.'

'That's a great idea,' Joy enthused. 'And if Angie had lenses she wouldn't have to wear her glasses, which would overcome that problem.'

'Can you get hold of some blue lenses, do you think, Lisa?'

'I should think so. You could probably get them from any opticians.'

'Good, then that's that problem overcome.' Angie paused, for once reluctant to go on.

'So now all we have to do is to choose which one of you two is going to be the guinea-pig,' Lisa said with a wicked grin as she looked at Angie and Gemma.

'Well, I would be quite willing to take part in the experiment, of course,' Angie began, 'but as I shall also be writing up all the notes it hardly seems fair that I should do both.'

'Nonsense,' said Gemma, 'what better than to have the results first hand when you write your thesis?'

'I can hardly be objective when I'm personally involved. And besides, it will take a great deal of work to make sure that the computer's instructions are carried out correctly. And you're the one who got a First in modern and mediaeval languages. You speak French better than I do.'

Gemma immediately started to argue and for a few minutes they exchanged heated reasons why neither of them were suitable for the task, while Lisa and Joy just sat there watching them and grinning like a couple of Cheshire cats until Lisa, as usual the peacemaker, stopped them.

'There's only one way to settle this. We'll just have to toss a coin for it.' She found a fifty-pence piece and knelt on the floor, the others gathering in a tight circle round her. 'Angie can call because it was her idea. The loser takes part in the experiment, okay?'

Angie and Gemma nodded, their faces tense.

Lisa spun the coin high in the air and Angie called, 'Heads!' Catching it deftly, Lisa covered the coin with her hand, enjoying the suspense in their faces as she deliberately made them wait. Then she slowly raised her hand. The Queen's head lay face upward.

'I won!' Angie exclaimed exultantly.

Gemma sank slowly back on to her heels, still staring at the coin, her face expressionless. Then she looked up at the picture of Paul Verignac. The others followed her gaze.

'I wonder if he's really as handsome as he looks?' Joy remarked.

Lisa said, 'What's more important, I wonder if he's really as good a lover as those girls said he was?'

'Well, we're about to find out—or at least, Gemma is about to find out for us.'

'Now wait a minute. Just how far do you expect me to go with this? If you think I'm. . . .'

But Angie interrupted her. 'We can go into all the finer points later, Gemma. Right now we have to make arrangements for setting up the experiment.'

'Yes, just how are we going to get near enough to Paul Verignac for him to meet Gemma?' Joy asked. 'We'll have to arrange something pretty startling or else he'll never notice her.'

'Thank you very much,' Gemma put in sardonically.

'It's all in the print-out,' Angie replied. 'He spends at least two months of every year skiing in the Alps at Zermatt. That's in the Valais region of southern Switzerland. He takes a chalet in the grounds of one of the luxury hotels for the entire winter so that he can entertain his friends and throw parties, that sort of thing.'

'We all know what kind of entertaining he does,' Gemma pointed out tartly. 'You've made that perfectly clear.'

Ignoring her, Angie continued, 'So I suggest that we go over to Switzerland as soon as we can after Christmas.' As Lisa had offered to finance the experiment, she added tactfully, 'Lisa, where do you think we should stay?'

'Well, if Gemma is going to maintain an aura of mystery, it might be better if we didn't stay at an hotel or pension where she might run into our victim—sorry, subject. So I think we ought to hire a chalet too, but a small private one a little out of the town.'

'Look, we can't expect you to pay for everything, Lisa,' Gemma objected. 'If we can't pay our way I don't think we ought to go.'

She was immediately shouted down and Lisa threw a cushion at her. 'Don't think you're going to get out of it that way, Gemma Kenyon. You said you were in on this and a promise is a promise. I'll pay our fares and for the hire of the chalet, plus any expenses incurred in the actual experiment, but otherwise we pay our own way, agreed?'

They agreed gratefully to this salve to their pride and got down to the serious business of arranging a date when they could all get away from their respective homes after the Christmas festivities. Eventually they decided on January the second.

'In the meantime we must get to work on Gemma,' Joy said sternly. 'Luckily we all know how to ski, but a few extra lessons at the ski-school will help, and we've got to get her a tan before we get to Zermatt.'

'And I'll get hold of a couple of wigs and Gemma must get contact lenses,' Lisa offered.

'Yes, and she can stand losing a few pounds too; Mr X likes girls with slim figures,' said Angie as she looked Gemma up and down critically.

Gemma glared at them. 'Do you mind not talking about me as if I were a dog you were getting ready for a show?' she said acidly.

'Not a show, more of a beauty contest,' Lisa advised her. 'And one in which you're going to be the rank outsider.' She gave an exaggerated sigh. 'So we'd better get started straightaway, we've got a long way to go,' and then fled as Gemma picked up the toasting fork and brandished it at her.

As they stepped on to the station platform, the crisp, cool mountain air gave them a lift like pure oxygen after the close fugginess of the train, packed full with holidaymakers. All around them people were struggling to unload their luggage and ski equipment, while others rushed ahead to commandeer one of the waiting horse-drawn taxis, for motor vehicles were banned in Zermatt until the spring sunshine finally melted the last of the winter snows.

The sun was shining now, giving the picturesque village with its wooden chalet houses and Alpine hotels, all encrusted with a thick layer of dazzlingly white snow, an almost fairytale appearance. Behind the village and completely dominating it rose the sheer, majestic peaks of the mountains, their harsh greyness hidden by the softening snow so that they looked like peaks of icing on a giant Christmas cake. Highest of them all was the Matterhorn; fourteen thousand, six hundred and fifty feet of solid rock that towered above them, outlined sharply against the vivid clear blue of the sky.

Gemma stared up at the peak with a sense of the awe one always feels when seeing the mountains again for the first time, but she was given little chance to stand and stare, because Angie was calling to her to help with the luggage. After a short wait they managed to get a horse-taxi and soon they were trotting along the road through the outskirts of the village, the sleigh bells on the horses' harness jingling merrily in the clear air. The gaily painted sleigh was upholstered in thick white fur and there were more fur rugs that they pulled closely around them to keep out the cold. They exclaimed excitedly as they travelled along, pointing out to each other the beginners on the nursery slopes and the more experienced skiers on the higher pistes.

'Look, that's where the railway to Gornergrat starts,' Lisa indicated. 'From there you can get a cable car up to Stockhorn; that's the highest point you can ski from.'

Lisa was the only one of them who had been to Zermatt before and was naturally making the most of her superior knowledge.

'Where's the hotel where Mr X is staying?' Angie asked.

'Oh, it's further back into the village. It doesn't look all that impressive from the outside, but it has an extremely good reputation for food and service, and in Switzerland that's really saying something.'

'Why do you keep calling him Mr X?' Gemma demanded.

'So that I can think of him objectively, of course,' Angie retorted. 'And you ought to as well. We have to look upon him as we would any other laboratory animal we were experimenting with.'

'It's hardly the same, Angie; rats and mice don't have human reactions,' Joy said reasonably.

'You'll just have to think of him as a human rat, Gemma,' Lisa told her laughingly.

'Oh, I think of him as that already,' she answered tartly.

They all laughed happily, their high spirits at being on holiday and the complete change in their surroundings going to their heads like strong wine.

The driver turned off the main road into a narrower street lined with small shops and business places where they stopped while Lisa went into an office to collect the keys for their rented chalet. Then the sleigh took them on into a road where large, opulent-looking private chalets lined either side. As the road began to climb uphill the houses became smaller, until they arrived almost at the top of the hill and pulled up outside a two-storied chalet, the lower storey of white-painted brickwork and the upper half of dark brown wood with an ornately carved balcony running across the front of the building.

'Here we are, the Chalet Domino. Our home from home for the next few weeks,' Lisa announced.

Laughing excitedly, they unloaded their luggage, while Joy, who was to be their treasurer, paid the driver. Lisa ceremoniously unlocked the door and then got pushed aside as they all rushed inside to explore.

'Hey, look at that fireplace!' Angie exclaimed, pointing to the ornate brick hearth. 'Mmm, I can't wait to light a fire in it.'

'Who gets the balcony rooms?' Gemma wanted to know. 'There are only two.'

After they had explored the neat little chalet with its small kitchen and bathroom, they brought in their luggage and then gathered in the big living-room where they tossed for the balcony rooms; Lisa and Gemma being the winners, with Joy and Angie having to share the large double room at the back of the house.

'The first thing we have to do is to go and buy some supplies,' Joy said practically.

'No, let's go and hire skis and boots first. I want to start skiing right away, don't you?' Lisa asked Gemma.

'Mm, great. And we can get our lift passes at the same time.'

'Do you three mind?' Angie said loudly. 'This is *not* a holiday. We're here to work. Admittedly we have to do all those things, but first of all we have to find Mr X and try to discover what he'll be doing for the next few days so that we can work out our plan of campaign. So I suggest we unpack and then go down to his hotel. It shouldn't be too difficult to find someone who works there who'll give us the information we want—a chambermaid or cleaner would do.'

'Why don't we split up?' Gemma suggested. 'You and Lisa can go and snoop round the hotel while Joy and I do the shopping.'

They agreed to this and within an hour they had unpacked and left the centrally heated warmth of the Chalet Domino to return to the village centre, but this time they were dressed in boots, gaily coloured and padded ski-suits, thick mittens and knitted snuggle hats to keep out the icy cold. The snow was such a novelty that at first they played in it like schoolgirls, throwing snowballs at one another and sliding down the sleigh tracks until they all ended in a laughing huddle on the ground, their breath turning to mist in the frosty air.

When they reached the busier part of the village, Angie made Gemma put on a pair of mirror-lensed sunglasses just in case they should happen to bump into Mr X. They found the hotel and agreed to meet in a bar in an hour's time so that they could all go and get fitted out with skis and boots. Joy and Gemma completed their shopping and got to the bar first, ordering drinks while they waited for the others. They had been sitting there for about twenty minutes when Lisa burst in.

'Come with me quickly. There's no time to lose!'

'What on earth...?' Gemma stared at her in amazement.

'*Come on!* Angie's waiting. There isn't time to explain.'

Hurriedly they picked up the bags of shopping and followed Lisa out into the street.

'Where are we going? What's the hurry?'

But Lisa didn't answer, just led them at a fast walk along the road until they came to a square that must have been some sort of garden in the summer. They saw Angie then; she was standing on a small raised platform and beckoning them to hurry. When they got to her, panting from their dash through the village, Gemma saw that Angie was standing by a telescope, one of those that was fixed in a stand in the ground and which the tourists could put money in to get a close-up view of the Alps.

'Quick, I'm running out of coins!'

'What is it?' Joy gasped.

'Mr X, of course,' Angie answered impatiently. 'He's just got off a chair lift and is walking towards the village.'

'Ooh, let me see!' Joy pushed in front and screwed her eye to the telescope. 'Which one?'

'He's wearing a black and red ski-suit. No hat. And he's with a girl in yellow.'

'Wait a minute. *Yes*, I've got him. Wow! What I wouldn't give to be a tall, willowy blonde. I say, that girl he's with is fabulously good-looking, Angie,' Joy added after a moment.

But Angie merely said hurriedly, 'Get out of the way, Joy, let Gemma have a look.'

Angie tried to pull Gemma forward to the telescope, but she hung back, feeling strangely reluctant to see the man they had come so far to find. But Angie pulled her forcibly forward and she unwillingly reached up to take off her sun-specs, part of her hoping that the money would run out or he would be gone before she could look. At first she could see only a crowd of brightly-clad people moving down the slope towards the village, but then, suddenly, a man came sharply into focus, seeming to fill the lens. Gemma recognised him at once from the magazine photograph. The same lean features and strong jaw, but now she could see that his hair was darker than she had thought, black rather than brown, and instead of the cynical expression there was now a small disdainful smile playing round his mouth as he looked down in contemptuous amusement at his companion. He stopped at a point where the road divided and said something. The girl pouted sexily up at him and he put his hands on her shoulders, drawing her to him, hunching over her as he pulled her close against him while he kissed her. Then he let her go, almost pushing her away, and laughing in her face before leaving her standing on the corner, looking forlornly after him.

The swine! Gemma thought as she watched. It was almost as if her thought had communicated itself to him, because he suddenly glanced up and seemed to be looking exactly in her direction. For a brief, startling second Gemma felt as a hunter must feel when he has his quarry lined up in the sights of his rifle and he savours the moment before he pulls the trigger. And that was what they were, she supposed, for hadn't they come here with the express intention of hunting this man down? But then he disappeared from view, hidden by the first of the houses.

Slowly Gemma straightened up and stepped back from the telescope. The others fired questions at her, but she hardly heard them. Her mind was full of the arrogant way he had brushed off the girl he had been with. Then she realised that she hadn't really noticed the girl at all; she had had eyes for no one but Mr X— no, not Mr X—Paul Verignac. Because he was too forceful a personality ever to be graded as an X factor. He was very much a man. But such a vain, narcissistic one that she rather thought she didn't so much mind making him their dupe, after all.

CHAPTER TWO

GEMMA came back to reality to find that the other three were all staring at her, Angie with a look of anxiety on her face.

'You haven't changed your mind now that you've seen him, have you?' she asked. 'You're not going to take a high moral tone or become pure-minded, and refuse to have anything to do with it?'

Gemma opened her mouth to speak, but before she could answer Joy said accusingly, 'She did on that other experiment we wanted to try. Do you remember? We were going to take a census to find out if girl students who were still virgins got higher marks than those who weren't, and Gemma wouldn't let us; she said it was immoral.'

'That's right,' Lisa joined in. 'She always has taken a holier-than-thou attitude whenever we want to try anything that's a bit daring. Personally I think it comes from reading all those mediaeval books, it gives her antiquated ideals.'

'When you've *quite* finished pulling me to pieces, perhaps you'd be interested to know that I haven't changed my mind,' Gemma retorted as she glared at them. 'On the contrary, I shall be quite happy to take part in the experiment. I think I'm going to enjoy using Paul Verignac. He looked just the type who needs to have the tables turned on him for a change.'

Lisa stared at her in pleased surprise. 'You've really got your dander up! Oh boy, there's nothing to beat Gemma when she gets her claws into someone. What did he do to make you so mad?'

Briefly Gemma explained, emphasising the way Paul Verignac had kissed the girl as if he was doing her a favour and then roughly got rid of her.

'Ugh, he sounds like a male chauvinist and then some. Angie, are you sure we picked the right man for our experiment? We don't want Gemma to get hurt,' Joy said rather worriedly.

'She won't get hurt as long as she doesn't let her emotions get involved,' Angie pointed out reasonably. 'And if Paul Verignac really is such a love-'em-and-leave-'em type and we manage to make him propose, then it will make the experiment an even bigger success. If we can get him, we can get anyone. What do you think, Gemma?'

'I agree,' she said at once. 'My only difficulty will be in not letting him see how much I despise him. And I think the sooner we start the better.'

'Great! Then let's do the rest of our errands and go back to the chalet to discuss our plan of campaign.'

But it was several hours later before they finally got down to business; it had taken them longer than they had expected to hire their ski gear and obtain their lift passes, and when they eventually got back to the Chalet Domino they were all hungry and decided to eat first. Lisa, who had been designated chief cook because she had once been friendly with someone who had taken a Cordon Bleu course, had found a fondue set in a cupboard and they had immediately decided to have a fondue party. What better way to start a holiday in Switzerland than with the Swiss national dish? They had great fun spiking chunks of bread on long forks and dipping them into the rich cheese sauce and kirsch mixture simmering in a copper dish kept hot above a small spirit stove, and the couple of bottles of wine they had bought to go with it helped to take their minds off more serious subjects.

It was quite late before Angie, as usual, brought them down to earth. 'Enough of this unseemly hilarity. We were going to work out our plan of campaign, remember? Come on, help me clear the table.' When they were sitting down again with only their notepads and pens in front of them, she got out the computer print-out and opened it. 'Now, I've already told you that Mr X likes women with an aura of mystery, and I think that what Gemma saw today emphasises that; he has no time for women who try to cling to him or make themselves too available.'

They all nodded, concentrating seriously now.

'The computer suggests that Mr X should be shown tantalising glimpses of Gemma before actually meeting her, so arousing his curiosity and his appetite for more. It said three sightings, because it rationalised that more would make her face familiar. Our job, of course, is to work out just how he's going to catch sight of her. Now, Lisa, I think you can help us here.'

'Yes. I spoke to several people at the hotel; most of them weren't a great deal of help, but then I talked to a horse-taxi driver who reports to Paul Verignac's hotel every morning in case he needs him. I pretended to be a goggle-eyed fan and slipped the man some money, and he was very forthcoming. He told me that Paul Verignac has a car, a red Lamborghini, that he keeps in that big car-park on the edge of the village. He said that he quite often takes him on the sleigh to the car-park in the mornings if Paul Verignac wants to go somewhere other than Zermatt for the day. I promised him more money if he let me know the next time he takes him there, and I think this man could probably be our most useful contact,' she added.

'Yes, it was he who told us where Paul Verignac had gone today so that we were able to spot him with the telescope,' Angie told them. 'Now what I suggest is this: the next time he uses his car we'll make our first move. On his way back to the village we'll arrange for Gemma to be skiing along parallel with the road for a while. We can set up some sort of signal so that she'll know when to go into action. Obviously he'll be going faster and will soon outdistance her—or perhaps we can set it near that part of the road where there's a deep bend—look, you can see it on the map—and then Gemma can ski away from the road. We don't want him to see her for more than a few minutes at the most.'

'She'll have to wear the blonde wig, of course, but what about the contact lenses? She won't get near enough for him to see her eyes, will she?' Joy asked.

Angie stuck out her bottom lip while she pondered the question. 'I think perhaps it would be better if she did. In fact I think she ought to start getting used to wearing them most of the time now, whenever she goes out anyway.'

'It should look great,' Joy, the most imaginative of them, enthused. 'Swishing along through the snow with her long blonde hair streaming in the breeze— a veritable ice-maiden. Any man would notice her, let alone a wolf like Paul Verignac.'

'That's the first stage of the experiment settled, then. First thing tomorrow we'll go up on the ski slopes so that Gemma can get some practice in. She's probably the best skier among us, but we don't want to take any chances. And in the afternoon we'd better go along the road and pick out a good spot for her to ski along, and also the areas where we can place the signallers in strategic hiding places so that we'll know when he's coming along.'

'If we have to hang around for him all day we'll be frozen,' Gemma pointed out.

'No need,' said Lisa with a grin. 'He usually tells the driver what time to come and pick him up from the car-park, so we only have to get in position about a half hour or so before then.'

Angie finished writing her notes and then looked up, her eyes excited. 'So it's about to begin.' She poured out the last of the wine and raised her glass. 'Let's drink to the success of our experiment.'

The others raised their glasses and clinked them against hers.

'To the ice-maiden experiment!' Lisa said with a grin.

For the third time Gemma pulled back the sleeve of her mitten to look at her watch. Over an hour already. Why didn't he come along? Her feet in the clip-on ski boots were getting cold and she lifted her legs to bang her feet on the ground to try to keep them warm. The driver of Paul Verignac's sleigh had phoned them earlier that day, the third day of their stay, to tell them that he had been instructed to pick him up at the car-park at four in the afternoon. Immediately they had gone into action, dressing Gemma up in the best ski-suit between them, a pale blue one with darker squares on the trousers giving a chequered effect. Her own chestnut mane they had pinned up and covered by the wig of luxurious long blonde hair that Lisa had bought from a theatrical costumiers. They also had another identical one in case they needed to use it as a spare while the first one was being set any time. Standing round Gemma and looking at her critically, they decided that her tan wasn't deep enough yet and so had applied instant tanning lotion. Then Lisa made her put in the contact lenses before making her up, emphasising her eyes and doing clever things to bring out her best features; her high cheekbones, straight nose, and finely arched brows. When they had finished Lisa led her to the mirror and stood back, waiting for her reaction.

Gemma simply stared. She looked so different that she wouldn't have recognised herself. The change in colouring and the pinker-toned lipstick that Lisa had used made her look younger and somehow more vulnerable. The sweep of her long, dark lashes and her dark eyebrows looked unusual and extremely attractive with the honey blonde of the wig. The fringe came almost down to her eyebrows and felt strange when she wasn't used to wearing one, for her own hair she always wore brushed off the face. She felt as if she wanted to keep pushing the fringe away from her eyes. Deep blue eyes that she felt didn't really belong to her; it was strange how much for granted you took your own face until something made you really look at it.

They had skied all the way from the chalet to the point in the road they had chosen the day before, so that Gemma could have extra practice, as she felt that just one morning wasn't really enough to regain her expertise and confidence. The spot they had picked out was about two miles from Zermatt, where the road went round a steep bend with fir trees at both ends of the bend and a long clear space in between. The idea was that Gemma should emerge from the trees as the car came along, ski across the open space while it drove round the bend, and then disappear into the far trees where the road straightened out again and where it was only about ten yards away, so giving Paul Verignac a brief, tantalising close-up, as Lisa described it.

Putting her sticks under her arm, Gemma banged her hands together and stamped her feet, clipped into the long skis. At least the wig kept her head warmer than any hat, she thought resignedly. She was standing among the fir trees, their branches heavy with snow, at the only point they could find which gave her a clear view of Joy, who was about five hundred yards away at the beginning of the stretch of trees, and who had a red scarf ready to wave at her when Paul Verignac's

car came in sight. Angie and Lisa were positioned further back along the road with a pair of binoculars.
They would signal to Joy who would wave once to tell
Gemma to get ready and a second time to tell her to
go. Which had seemed all very well at the time, but
meant that Gemma had to stand in the same place, not
daring to move in case she missed the signal, her limbs
and extremities getting more numb without the heat
of the sun to warm her.

A flickering movement caught her eye and she
blinked. Darn these lenses, they were making her eyes
water. She looked again and saw that Joy was waving
the scarf vigorously. Gemma waved back and got in
position facing the slope, her sticks in her hands ready
to push off. Her heart began to pump excitedly as she
looked back over her shoulder, waiting for the second
signal. After a few minutes that seemed like ages it
came. Gemma took a deep breath and launched herself
out of the cover of the last few trees and across the open
ground.

At first she couldn't see the car and thought that she
had mistimed it, but then she heard the deep, expensive sound of the engine and glimpsed the flash of
brilliant red paintwork as it came fast down the road.
She pushed her sticks into the snow to push her along
faster so that she could keep parallel with it. The skis
sang crisply over the frosted snow and the sun felt warm
on her face, she could feel the breeze created by her
momentum blowing the blonde hair out behind her as
she strove to keep abreast of the sports car, which was
negotiating the long bend much faster than she had
expected. For a second she caught a glimpse of the
driver's face looking in her direction, but then she returned her attention to the task in hand, concentrating solely on getting to the fir trees at the same time as
he did.

They were coming nearer now, thank goodness, one
more burst of effort should do it. The sound of the car
was very close on her right, although she couldn't see
it unless she turned her head. As she did so the breeze
blew the fringe into her eyes; impatiently she raised her
hand to brush it aside. But her glove dislodged one of
the lenses slightly and she automatically closed her eyes,
screwing them up against the sudden pain. She tried to
bring her skis round to a stop, but her legs were still
almost numb, and then one of her sticks slipped from
her grasp. Managing to open one eye, Gemma found
herself heading straight for the road, the roar of the
powerful engine seemingly almost on top of her.

Desperately she tried to stop, but her left ski caught a
bump and she went over, tumbling in a ball of flailing
arms and legs and skis until she fell with a thud on to
the hard, compacted-snow surface of the road. Behind
her there was the deafening sound of the car and the
shriek of tyres as the brakes were applied at full force.
Too terrified to move, Gemma lay in the road with her
arms over her head and waited for the impact. She felt
something brush her sleeve and then the engine cut and
there was a sudden silence, almost more deafening than
the noise in its complete contrast.

Still Gemma didn't move. She couldn't believe that
the car had missed her, it had been so close. Vaguely
she heard the car door open and then quick footsteps
covered the few feet towards her.

'Are you hurt? I didn't touch you, did I?' Paul Verignac spoke in French, his voice sharp, as he came to
kneel beside her.

Rather dazedly Gemma sat up and stared at him as
he loomed over her, his face white beneath his tan.

'N-no.' Although she had understood him perfectly,
she was so stunned by fright that she answered him in
English and he immediately switched to that language,

which he spoke with hardly any accent.

'Did I hit you?'

'No.'

'Not even touch you?'

'No.' He helped her to her feet and she brushed the snow off her suit with unsteady hands.

'You're quite sure you're all right?'

'Yes, I think so—thank you.'

He let out a breath of relief as colour came back into his face, and Gemma saw that he had been as shaken as she was. The anxiety left his voice and was replaced by anger.

'Then would you mind telling me what the hell a rank amateur like you was doing skiing so close to the road? The place for beginners is on the nursery slopes! Because of your crass stupidity you came damn near to getting yourself killed, and if you had it would have been your own fault!'

His anger brought Gemma back to earth with startling abruptness. She lifted her head to see him glaring down at her, his grey eyes as cold and hard as the snow-capped mountains. The reaction from the shock of the near-accident brought a rush of emotions, the uppermost being fury at his high-handed tone.

'How dare you swear at me? And I am *not* a beginner! Something went in my eye and made me lose my balance, that's all. And anyway you'd no right to be travelling at that speed on snow. This is an Alpine road, not the Le Mans circuit!'

There was a short silence and Gemma had the satisfaction of seeing him look momentarily disconcerted before he said, 'I did have snow tyres on and the car is fitted with extremely good brakes, luckily for you.'

The patronising tone of that last remark only served to increase Gemma's anger. 'You were still driving much too fast. I bet you were doing sixty.'

'Possibly I was.'

'What?' she almost squeaked as her voice rose in fury.

'Kilometres—not miles.'

'Oh.'

'And I'm damned if I see why I should stand here and justify myself to an idiot like you. As it is, it's no thanks to you that I haven't wrecked my car.'

Guiltily Gemma turned and saw that his beautiful sports car was slewed across the road at an acute angle, its front offside wheel right up the bank and buried in the loose snow.

'Is it very badly damaged?'

'I haven't had time to look.' He sprang lightly up the bank and went round to the other side of the car to inspect it. 'No, it seems to be all right.'

Gemma gave a sigh of relief; she had envisaged having to pay a huge bill for repairs. Vaguely she looked round for her skis and sticks and saw them scattered on the road a few feet away. Slowly she went to pick them up, and as she did so noticed a tear in the sleeve of her suit. So the car had touched her, after all. The nearness of her escape came flooding back and she sat down abruptly on the bank. Behind her she heard the engine of the car start up and watched as Paul Verignac backed it carefully on to the road again and straightened it up. He got out again and came over to her. For the first time she really looked at him. He was wearing a brown suede suit over a tan polo-necked sweater and seemed very tall and masculine as he stood beside her. He was, she realised, an extremely macho man, his air of arrogant virility as natural to him as breathing. Suddenly Gemma remembered the girl he had brushed off and her dislike of him hardened.

He spoke to her with reluctant concern. 'You're very pale. Are you sure you're not hurt?'

'My legs feel rather shaky, that's all. I expect it's

shock or something. I'll be all right in a minute.'

'Give me your ski-gear. I'll put it on the roof rack and drive you to Zermatt.'

'No!'

He frowned. 'Do you mean you're not staying at Zermatt?'

'No—I mean, yes, I am staying at Zermatt, but you don't have to take me.'

'Nonsense, you're in no state to get back under your own steam.' He reached for her sticks and skis, but Gemma hung on to them.

'Thank you, but I'm perfectly all right now and I prefer to make my own way back.'

'So that you can fall under another car, or break your neck when you trip over your own skis or go down a crevasse? You're not fit to be allowed out alone.'

Stung, Gemma retorted, 'Well, I'd rather risk those things than go in a car with a lousy driver like you!'

He glared at her in furious bafflement. 'Don't be so silly, can't you see that you're in no state to be left on your own? Are you going to get in the car or do I have to pick you up and put you in it?'

Taking hold of one of the ski sticks, Gemma held it defensively. 'I don't accept rides from strange men. Now will you please take your rotten car and go away and leave me alone?'

Paul Verignac stood gazing down at her angrily, his hands on his hips, his mouth set in a grim line. He muttered something under his breath. 'Very well, mademoiselle, on your own stupid little head be it.' Then he turned abruptly and walked back to the car without a backward glance. Starting up the engine, he drove off down the road.

Morosely Gemma watched him go, noticing sourly that he was driving much slower. When the car had driven out of sight, she looked back at the road unbelievingly. There was nothing to show for her narrow escape except the dent in the snow bank where the car had mounted it and the skid marks on the hard-packed road where he had braked and spun the car round to avoid her. As she looked she realised just how closely he had missed her, and, being a car driver herself, she saw that he must have reacted with split-second awareness to have avoided her. In fact, if Paul Verignac hadn't been such a good driver it would have been a completely different story. Which realisation didn't make her feel any better at all.

Feeling slightly sick, she staggered to a nearby tree and dropped down in the snow to lean against its trunk. Putting her hand up to her head that had begun to throb, she felt the wig and remembered it for the first time. Presumably it had stayed in place during her tumble—probably because of all the hairpins Lisa had used to anchor it against the breeze—because Paul Verignac hadn't seemed to notice anything amiss. She supposed that the lenses were all right too; they felt okay. Unless one had come out completely and she had confronted him with one blue eye and one brown. This thought made her giggle rather hysterically, and then she cried a little as shock and reaction hit her.

But after a few minutes she resolutely blew her nose and sniffed hard. She was lucky to be alive, wasn't she? So what was there to cry about? The only thing she had to worry about now was how to tell the girls that she had completely wrecked the experiment. The tantalising glimpse that Paul Verignac was supposed to have had of her had turned into an angry confrontation, and there was no way now that they would ever succeed in their hopes. Not that there had ever really been any chance from the beginning, she admitted to herself; Paul Verignac just wasn't the type to let any woman trap him into marriage. If and when he ever

decided he wanted a wife, he would choose one who
would suit his purposes and then inform her of the
honour he was doing her, Gemma decided caustically.

She heard a shout and turned to wave as the others
appeared at the other side of the slope. She was thank-
ful that they had had some distance to cover and hadn't
seen the fiasco she had made of things. They came
crisply across the snow, Lisa and Joy in the rear so
that Angie reached her first and plopped down on the
snow beside her, her cheeks glowing from the exercise
and her eyes bright with excitement.

'How did it go? Did he see you, do you think?'

'Oh, yes, he saw me all right.'

The others came up, panting, and joined them.

'Gemma says he saw her.'

'Oh, great,' Lisa enthused. 'Did you actually see him
look at you? That's marvellous,' she went on when
Gemma nodded, giving her no time to speak. 'Now
we'll be able to plan part two of the experiment. We'll
work it out tonight.'

Guilt kept Gemma silent; it was so hard to find words
to tell them when she knew the disappointment she
would create. They all began to laugh and talk excitedly, completely ignoring her, and as Gemma looked
at their bright faces she knew that she just couldn't
spoil it for them, especially Angie, who had spent weeks
finding out all the information and programming the
computer. They would be nice about it, she knew, but
nevertheless it would ruin their holiday before it had
hardly begun. Surely it wouldn't do any harm to let
them go on thinking that everything was going to plan?
The computer had specified that Paul Verignac was
supposed to see her three times before she actually got
to meet him, and as it was now more than certain that
if he did see her he would ignore her completely, cut
her dead, it didn't seem to Gemma that going on with

the experiment that far would be too deceitful. And after that, if they somehow arranged a meeting she could just pretend that he hadn't wanted to know— not that there would be any pretence about it after this afternoon, she thought drily. The girls would probably be willing to accept that and put the failure of the experiment down to human irrationality rather than her own stupidity, and they would all be able to enjoy the rest of their time in Zermatt as an ordinary holiday, instead of worrying about their stupid experiment, which she considered doomed from the start anyhow.

Thinking along these lines made her feel better, but she was still lost in thought when Angie's voice made her jump guiltily.

'Gemma, have you been crying? Your eyes are all wet.' Angie was peering at her closely.

'Of course not. It's these lenses; they make my eyes water. Can I take them out now?'

'I suppose so, but for heaven's sake don't lose them.'

'It's all right, the box is in my pocket.' Gemma stowed the lenses safely away and fastened on her skis. 'Come on, I'll race you back to Zermatt. Last one at the chalet does the washing-up!'

The others gave a howl of protest as she dug her sticks into the snow and set off towards the village, then they came flying after her, their laughter echoing through the mountains.

Angie wanted to get down to working out the next part of their plan straightaway, but Gemma put her foot down and insisted they have an evening off, so they all dolled themselves up in their best après-ski clothes, Gemma refusing point blank to wear the wig and lenses, and took a sleigh down to 'Le Village de la Poste' which was reputed to be the best disco in town. Four such good-looking girls weren't left alone for long

and they soon became friendly with a group of Danish
students, some of whom already had girls with them.
They drank the local wine, danced a lot, and laughed
even more, and to Gemma it was a great relief to relax
and try to forget about the disturbing encounter with
Paul Verignac. But somehow she couldn't put him completely out of her mind; the memory of the accident
and the cold anger in his eyes when he had told her
just what he had thought of her still sent shivers down
her spine. She tried to give her full attention to Kurt,
the tall, fair-haired young Dane who had immediately
singled her out. He spoke extremely good English and
was very flattering, but she found that she was in no
mood for even a mild flirtation. She still felt rather
guilty about deceiving the others, but there was no
going back now. Determinedly she pushed all other
thoughts to the back of her mind and gave herself to
the present.

The young men escorted them home and made a date
for them all to go skiing together the following morning. They originally asked the girls to spend the day
with them, but Angie reminded them drily that they
had other things to do. Kurt tried to draw Gemma to
one side to kiss her goodnight, but she playfully fended
him off until he laughed and let her go.

Quite a crowd of them set off the next morning to
take the two-carriage mountain train on the rack railway up to Gornergrat. They piled their ski gear into
the open wagon at the rear and then climbed into one
of the carriages, their brightly coloured ski clothes
dazzling to the eye. Slowly the train climbed higher,
twisting in long bends up the side of the mountain,
until Zermatt looked like a Lilliputian village far below them. There were several stops on the way up, but
they stayed on the train until they reached the end of
the line. At ten thousand feet the change in the tem-

perature and air was dramatic, when they stepped out
of the train the cold seemed to go deep into their lungs
with the first breath they took, but the sun was shining,
making them all feel invigorated and alive.

From here they had the choice of taking a chair-lift
further up the mountain to Stockhorn or of skiing
down an intermediate run to Findeln, a drop of nearly
four thousand feet. After some discussion they decided
on the latter course as they were not all experienced
skiers and some of the others thought the run from
Stockhorn might be too much for them. Somebody suggested they have a hot drink first, so they went to the
nearby restaurant where lots of people were sitting outside drinking coffee and soaking up the sun, a forest of
ski sticks and skis stuck in the snow in front of the
tables.

The sun felt wonderful and Gemma soon took off
her hat to let her hair fall free round her shoulders.
Shouts of laughter echoed up from the nursery slopes
further down the mountain where the beginners
laboured. Others had hired toboggans and were having
great fun hurtling over the snow at breakneck speed,
often falling off in the process. Above their heads the
Matterhorn dominated the skyline, looking almost over-
powering in its nearness, and in the distance a helicopter, painted bright orange and white, flew noisily by,
taking those rich enough to afford it from the heliport
just outside Zermatt high up into the mountains, so
cutting out the often tedious waits for cable-cars and
lifts.

From where they were sitting they could see both the
railway and the start of the chair-lift. Another train
came in and Gemma watched idly as the passengers
dispersed, some to the restaurant, others to the start of
the ski run or chair-lift. Suddenly she found herself
stiffening as she saw a man in a black and red ski-suit

stepping crisply across to the chair-lift. Surely it couldn't be? But there was no mistaking Paul Verignac, his autocratic bearing rather than his height making him stand out from those around him. For a moment he glanced in their direction and Gemma sat staring, her cup frozen in mid-air. She must have made a strangled sound because Angie looked at her sharply and then followed the direction of her eyes.

'It's all right, he won't recognize you without the wig,' she hissed at her.

And indeed he had already looked away and was seating himself in the lift. Gemma slowly let out her breath, not in the least surprised to find that her hand was shaking as she at last raised the coffee cup to her mouth and took a big gulp of the hot, strong liquid. Shortly afterwards they all set off towards the head of the ski run, but Angie pulled her to one side.

'Seeing Paul Verignac up here has given me an idea. We must find out how often he comes here.'

'What idea?' Gemma asked warily.

But Angie didn't have time to explain because Kurt came up to Gemma to help her with her skis and there was no further chance to discuss it that morning. The run down to Findeln was fantastic, the best skiing Gemma had ever experienced, and from there they took a chair-lift high over another nursery slope to Sunnegga and skied down the comparatively easy run that took them almost all the way back to Zermatt. They had a drawn-out lunch in a village restaurant, but Gemma felt far too tense and anxious about what Angie might have in mind to really enjoy it. She could hardly wait to say goodbye to the others and to be on their own. But even then Angie wouldn't say anything until they got back to the chalet. By then Lisa and Joy had gathered that there was something in the wind and were just as keen to find out.

'Come on, Angie, stop being so darn mysterious and tell us what ploy you've thought up,' Lisa commanded.

'Well, it was seeing Paul Verignac using the chair-lift that gave me a really brilliant idea,' Angie told them with complete lack of modesty. 'We need another way for him to see Gemma without coming too close, and what better way than for him to pass her on the chair-lift, him going up and Gemma coming down?' she finished triumphantly.

'It *is* a good idea,' Joy acknowledged. 'But we'd have to get the timing exactly right. How can we find out when he'll use a chair-lift again, though? Just because he used one today it doesn't mean he'll necessarily use the same one again for some time—it could be weeks.'

'We could ask his sleigh driver again,' Lisa suggested.

They went on enlarging the idea more fully, but Gemma didn't give them her full attention; she was too busy working out how it would affect her in the light of their first traumatic encounter. On the face of it the idea seemed quite safe; she definitely wouldn't come close enough to Paul Verignac to have to speak to him, and it would be too far away for the others to see if he ignored her completely. Yes, she rather thought it would do. Gemma switched back on to the others and found that they had agreed on everything except the minor details that might crop up.

'That's decided, then,' Angie was saying. 'Tomorrow morning we'll have Gemma positioned in a horse-taxi in the village square and we'll arrange for Paul Verignac's driver to give us a signal telling us which lift he's taking. Whichever way he goes, he's almost certain to take a chair-lift, so we just have to make sure that Gemma gets to the top before he does. If he's heading for the car-park we'll call the whole thing off until the next day, of course.'

'Won't it look peculiar if she's coming *down*?' Lisa asked. 'Everybody skis down.'

'It might make him wonder,' Angie admitted. 'But it does mean that he'll be sure to notice her, so I think that's to the good.'

'What if I'm too far ahead of him?' Gemma objected. 'I might get down before he starts coming up. And I don't want to meet him face to face,' she added feelingly.

'Hm. I suppose we'll have to arrange some sort of signal again. Joy can stand at the bottom of the lift and wave her hat or something at you when he gets on.'

Lisa pointed out, 'In some places there are two lifts going up from the same spot. How will we know which one he takes?'

Angie consulted the map. 'Well, obviously one of us will have to follow him and when we see which way he's going she can telephone ahead to the restaurant so that Gemma can ski across to the top of whichever lift he's on. None of those that start off from the same point finish up too far apart and Gemma should have no difficulty in cutting across and getting on the lift before he gets to the top. Luckily there are four of us, so we should be able to cover all eventualities.'

The next morning found Gemma, her disguise covered by a hat and mirror specs just in case Paul Verignac should see her too soon, positioned in a sleigh in the village square not far from his hotel with Angie and Joy. Angie had told the driver that they were playing a joke and he had immediately entered into the spirit of the thing. He had a pair of strong chestnut horses who fretted impatiently to be away. They had been waiting for some time because Angie was worried in case they missed him, but Lisa was still loitering as unostentatiously as possible on the distant street corner where she could see the entrance to the hotel.

'I bet he went to a party or something last night and is still sleeping it off,' Joy said sullenly as she rubbed her arms to keep warm.

The others ignored her; Joy was notorious for hating to get up in the mornings and was always sulky for a few hours if made to get up a fraction earlier than usual.

'Look, Lisa's waving!' Angie said suddenly, and they all peered at the corner. 'Both arms to tell us to get ready. Acknowledge it, Joy, you've got the scarf.'

Obediently Joy pushed aside the fur rug and stood up to wave.

'She should get the signal from the driver any second. Get ready, we must get the number right,' Angie told them tersely. 'No, not you, Gemma, keep your back to the road in case he comes by.'

Joy and Gemma looked at each other, then said together, 'Yes, ma'am,' with extreme sarcasm.

But Angie was too excited to notice. 'Here it comes! Left arm—one, two, three waves. That means the third lift to the west of the village. Great! That's the chair-lift up to Sunnegga. Just what we need.' Quickly she gave the instruction to the driver and they set off at a fast trot towards the outskirts of the village.

Against orders, Gemma glanced back and was in time to see Paul Verignac's sleigh turn into the road behind them. She just prayed that there wouldn't be too big a queue for the lift and that she would be able to draw well ahead of him. Lisa had slipped his driver a hundred francs and he had promised to delay the drive as much as possible so that they could get ahead.

With some relief they found that there was only a short line of skiers waiting for the chair-lift and the second sleigh wasn't even in sight by the time they had put on their skis and waited their turn.

'You and Joy go on ahead,' Angie directed. 'I'll stay here and keep watch for him. Give me the scarf, Joy, so that I can signal. Don't forget to take off the hat and glasses when you get to the top, Gemma.'

Gemma was about to make a sharp retort but bit it back. She and Joy climbed on to the slowly moving lift and it soon left the ground behind and began to carry them upward over the pine trees, their branches bending under the weight of the snow. Joy had to keep craning her neck round to watch Angie, but the lift seemed to keep going on for ever: one thousand feet, two thousand, before they at last came to the top and could slide off.

'I can't see Angie any more.' Joy said distractedly. 'Can you make her out?'

'No, it's much too far away, and there seem to be a lot of people down there now.'

'We should have brought some binoculars. Angie will never forgive us if we botch things up,' Joy wailed.

Gemma flushed and looked hurriedly away. 'Paul Verignac's probably coming up by now. I'd better go down.' She took off the sunglasses and slipped them into her pocket, then took off the hat, being careful not to dislodge the wig. 'Do I look all right? No dark hair showing?'

'No, you look fine. Good luck!'

'Thanks.' Gemma made her way to the turn-round point of the lift and got on again. Soon the sounds of human voices were left behind and a silence closed in around her from the stark mountains. They were majestic, magnificent, freaks of nature formed by a force so powerful that man could only guess at its strength, and yet mankind turned them into a playground in both winter and summer, climbing them because they were there, for if men could conquer the mountains then perhaps they felt, just for a moment, that they could also triumph over the forces of nature that had put them there. Until, of course, the mountains decided to teach humanity a small, playful lesson and sent avalanches thundering down to destroy whole villages in their path and jog men into remembering just how puny they really were.

Perhaps the aura of the mountains got to her, for she felt almost breathless with anticipation, her heart hammering as she anxiously scanned the chairs coming up towards her just a few feet away. Her second encounter with the forceful Paul Verignac was about to take place, and she felt as tense and nervous as a schoolgirl on her first date.

CHAPTER THREE

EVERY chair on the lift was taken and Gemma expected to see Paul Verignac come into view at any moment, so she tried to pretend that she was looking at the scenery while at the same time sneaking quick looks sideways to spot him as soon as he came in sight. There were many men on the lift and most of them gave her appreciative glances, but as she got lower and lower she abandoned the pretence of enjoying the view and concentrated entirely on looking for him. Perhaps he was wearing a different ski-suit today and she had missed him. But somehow she thought no one could pass Paul Verignac by without noticing him. As the lift descended into the valley she could make out Angie standing at the bottom and she rushed over as soon as Gemma got out of the chair.

'Where is he? Did I miss him?' Gemma asked anxiously.

'No, he hasn't turned up yet. There's been no sign of him.'

'Oh, no! Don't tell me all this has been for nothing?'

'Perhaps his driver gave the wrong signal, or else Lisa misunderstood him,' Angie said distractedly.

'What are you going to do, call the whole thing off?' Despite herself, Gemma couldn't help a hopeful note creeping into her voice.

'Certainly not!' Angie returned sharply. 'We'll give him some more time—he might have got delayed. You'd better go back up, Gemma, and wait for my signal. You shouldn't have come down until I'd given it anyway.'

'Unfortunately,' Gemma answered tartly, 'we can't see you from the top, it's too far away. So I suppose I shall just have to keep riding up and down the lift.'

Worriedly Angie answered, 'No, you can't do that. There are lots of people waiting now and you might get behind him in the queue.'

'But he'd see me when I got off,' Gemma reasoned.

'Not necessarily. He might be talking or looking the other way. And there's always the possibility that if he did see you he might try to pick you up. And we don't want that yet.'

'No, we certainly don't,' Gemma agreed, imagining the sarcastic greeting she would probably receive. 'What are you going to do, then?'

'You'd better go up straightaway and then send Joy down. When she's halfway she can signal to me and I'll get on. That way we should always have someone in sight of both you and the start of the lift so that we can pass on the signals. Yes, I think that's best,' Angie finished, pleased with her strategy. 'You go ahead and tell Joy.'

Resignedly Gemma stood in line and waited for the lift again, having to share the double seat with an Italian youth who tried to make a date with her the whole way up, until she snubbed him forcefully in his own language and he got off at the top to stalk away in a manner of hurt dignity—which wasn't easy on skis. Gemma gave Joy the message and watched until she became a small dot in the distance. Angie came up and said tersely, 'No sign of him yet,' before going back down again.

Twice more this happened and Gemma began to get extremely bored and cold just standing around. What anyone watching them from the restaurant must think of their antics she hated to imagine. As usual there were lots of people seated outside drinking the

delicious morning coffee; she could smell the aroma of
it on the breeze. Several times she glanced longingly towards the restaurant, and when Angie had just started
the descent for the third time she made up her mind.
Taking off her skis, she dug them in the snow and went
into the restaurant; she was going to have a coffee whatever Angie said about it! She could drink it outside
where she could see the lift, and if the signal came she
could always carry her skis across her knees on the
chair.

Luckily there was only a short queue and she soon
had a steaming mug of coffee and a gooey cream cake
balanced on a small tray to take outside. Turning to
walk back through the restaurant, she suddenly found
that the steam had fogged up her contact lenses and she
couldn't see a thing. Her leg caught against a chair
and in turning to avoid it she bumped into someone
who had just come into the building. She felt the tray
fall from her hand and heard a sharp exclamation in
a male voice.

Blinking hard, she managed to clear the lenses and
looked up rather owlishly to find Paul Verignac looking grimly down at her, his mouth set in a thin line
as he strove to control his anger. Slowly, reluctantly,
Gemma let her eyes travel downwards. He had unzipped the anorak he was wearing and under it he had
a pure white and very expensive-looking polo-neck
sweater. At least it *had* been white—now it had a great
brown stain all down the front of it, and also a large
smeary blob of what looked like cream from her cake.

'Oh, no!' Gemma said faintly. 'I—I'm most terribly
sorry. I couldn't see where I was going and I....'

'A habit you seem to have, mademoiselle,' he interrupted sarcastically. He picked up some paper napkins
from a nearby table and started to wipe off the cream.

'Oh, here, let me do that.' Gemma tried to take them

TAB
FIC
W48i

from him, but as she did so touched his hand, which so unnerved her that she only succeeded in getting some of the cream on his anorak as well.

Deliberately he took the napkins back from her and cleaned up the sweater as much as he could himself.

'I'm afraid it's ruined,' Gemma said unhappily. 'If you'll let me know how much it cost I'll give you a cheque so that you can replace it,' she offered, mentally reviewing her possessions to think what she could sell to raise the money.

Paul Verignac raised an eyebrow, a slight curl of sardonic amusement on his lips. 'It's irreplaceable; the wool was spun from sheep of a mountain breed that has now died out completely.'

For some unaccountable reason this angered her. 'Any department store sweater would have served the same purpose,' she pointed out rather cuttingly. 'You didn't *have* to massacre a herd of sheep.'

'I don't frequent department stores.'

'I bet you don't, you snob,' Gemma retorted, his high-handed manner getting her back up. 'And I bet that if you'd been looking where you were going you wouldn't have knocked into me. You were probably too busy keeping your nose in the air, so that you wouldn't be polluted by the hoi-polloi,' she added nastily.

To her annoyance this didn't have the desired effect of making him angry, instead he merely folded his arms and looked down at her derisively. 'The common reaction I would expect from one of your type.'

Gemma put her hands on her hips and glared up at him. 'And just what is *that* supposed to mean?'

'Simply that whenever anyone with an outsize inferiority complex feels themselves to be threatened they immediately react by becoming belligerent and rude.'

'Well, of all the nerve!' Gemma exploded. 'Let me tell you, you'd make a lousy psychologist. Because I certainly don't feel inferior to you—it's the other way round. In my book anyone who *flaunts* his money just isn't worth knowing!' Angrily she pushed past him. 'And in future will you please keep out of my way?'

He gave her a mocking bow. 'A request I shall be most happy to agree to, mademoiselle.'

Lifting her chin, Gemma tossed her hair disdainfully and strode out of the restaurant, completely spoiling the effect by slipping on the icy snow outside and almost falling on her face. She didn't turn her head to see if he'd seen and was laughing at her, but walked more carefully to where she had left her skis and banged her feet down hard to engage the clips, which relieved her feelings a little.

Still smarting from the encounter, she went over it angrily in her mind, thinking too late of all the things she would have liked to say to the insufferable man. It wasn't until she saw Joy's familiar figure come into sight on the chair-lift that she realised that she'd messed everything up for the second time. Her face flushed crimson with guilt. Oh lord, not again! But how was she to know that he would suddenly appear in the restaurant? She certainly hadn't received any signal from the others that he was on the way up, and he had followed her so closely into the building that if he had been that near to the top she would have seen him on the lift. So where on earth had he come from? And what was more important, was she going to confess to the others?

By the time Joy got to the top Gemma had made up her mind. She signalled to her friend to stay on the lift and jumped into the seat beside her.

'We can call it off,' she told Joy. 'He's here at Sunnegga.'

'What? But how did he get here? He definitely didn't come up the lift.'

'I don't know how he got here; I only know he's here,' Gemma answered shortly.

Eagerly, Joy asked, 'Did he see you?'

'Yes, I saw him coming into the restaurant and passed him on my way out,' Gemma replied, her fingers crossed inside her mittens.

'That's fantastic! He didn't try to pick you up or anything?'

'No, he definitely didn't try to pick me up,' said Gemma with utmost certainty.

'Angie will be really pleased, even if things didn't work out exactly as she planned. We'd better try to signal her so that she doesn't get back on the lift and have a wasted journey.'

Joy immediately began to wave her scarf vigorously, much to the amusement of the people going up the lift, until Gemma said irritably, 'Do you have to do that? Angie can't possibly see you yet, you know.'

Joy looked at her in some astonishment. 'What's the matter?'

'I'm freezing cold and I'm hungry, that's what's the matter. It wasn't any fun standing about all that time.'

'Well, it wasn't much fun for us either,' Joy said reasonably. 'There's quite a wind cutting across the valley and it was freezing on the chairs too.'

Gemma was immediately contrite. 'I'm sorry, Joy. It's just that this whole thing is becoming ridiculous. What seemed like a feasible idea back in England is beginning to take on all the aspects of a farce. How could we have seriously believed that any man would fall for a girl just because a computer said he would? It's laughable! Especially when you see Paul Verignac close to. He's just an arrogant sexist. We haven't got a hope in hell of carrying this thing through, and as far

as I'm concerned the sooner we call it off the better,'
she finished vehemently.

Joy looked at her in dismay but wisely refrained
from saying anything, concentrating instead on catching Angie's attention before she got on the lift again.
When they got to the bottom, Joy told her what had
happened and the poor girl didn't know whether to be
pleased that Gemma had seen Paul Verignac or sorry
that her plan had misfired.

'What I can't understand is how he got up there,' she
said for the third time as they hoisted their skis on their
shoulders and started back towards the village.

But the mystery was solved when they met Lisa
hurrying in a horse-taxi to meet them. 'Paul Verignac's
driver phoned me at the chalet and said that he'd
stopped at a ski-goods shop for some bindings he'd left
to be repaired and which weren't quite ready, so he had
to wait for them,' she explained. 'That made him too
late to meet the people he had been intending to spend
the day with, so instead of taking the lift he made the
driver take him straight to the heliport and took a helicopter up to Unter Rothorn. He must have skied all
the way down to Sunnegga.'

'His driver might have come and told us!' Angie
exclaimed in annoyance.

'He did, but you weren't there.'

'I must have been on the lift. And of course he doesn't
know Joy even if she was there. Still, never mind, at
least we achieved our purpose.' Angie turned to Gemma
to question her about the meeting, but Joy hastily intervened, raising her eyebrows expressively and looking
warningly in Gemma's direction.

Angie got the message and talked about other things
until they got back to the Chalet Domino, but then lost
no time in getting Joy on her own to find out what had
happened. Gemma shut herself in her room and let

them get on with it. Rather wearily she changed out
of her ski clothes into ordinary slacks, taking off her disguise with relief. As far as she was concerned the morning had been completely wasted; they should have been
enjoying themselves instead of running after Paul Verignac in an absurd attempt to prove Angie's theory.
And now she had only made the situation worse than
ever. Glumly she walked downstairs to the sitting-room.

The others stopped talking as soon as she came in,
which didn't help any, but then Angie jumped up and
said over-brightly, 'We thought we would go out to
lunch today, Gemma. Why don't you choose where to
go?'

'Why me?' Gemma asked ungraciously as she flopped
into an armchair.

'We tossed for it and you won. Come on, Gemma,
snap out of it. Choose a place to eat. We've already
rung for a taxi,' Lisa told her.

They started to coax and chivvy her out of her
gloomy mood and Gemma realised that she wouldn't
have any peace until she did what they wanted. 'Okay,
okay,' she said at last, raising her hands in resignation.
'Pass me the list of restaurants and I'll pick one.' She
gave it only a cursory glance. 'Here we are, the Slalom.
We can try that dish called *raclette* that everyone keeps
talking about.'

The others were all very cheerful and nice to her for
the rest of the day, and Gemma was fully aware that
they were buttering her up to make her go on with the
experiment, and her feelings alternated between annoyance and guilt. She would have given anything to just
call off the whole thing and enjoy the holiday, but she
realised they wouldn't be satisfied until they had seen
for themselves that it had failed. Which meant that she
would have to go along with them for a while longer.
Though the thought of having to face Paul Verignac

again filled her with dread. She knew she had a temper, but usually she managed to keep it well under control. Paul Verignac, however, seemed to have the ability to make her lose it at the drop of a hat. Probably because he was so autocratic.

By that evening Gemma couldn't stand having the girls be kind and solicitous to her any longer.

'All right, you might as well tell me. I know you've got something lined up; you'd never be this sweet-natured for so long if you didn't want me to do something—and something that you know I won't like, so let's have it,' she commanded.

The others glanced at each other and by tacit consent Lisa spoke for them. 'We know you've never been really keen on the idea, Gemma, and that it hasn't been any fun so far, waiting in the cold and everything, so we thought that for the third part of the experiment we would change all that and this time let you go somewhere that's warm.'

'That's big of you,' Gemma said drily, then added suspiciously, 'Just where have you in mind?'

'The swimming pool at his hotel,' Angie said promptly. 'Paul Verignac goes there for a work-out every day. You could wear your bikini and pass him as he was going in.'

'Yes, and you'd be able to show off your tan,' Joy joined in as they all looked at her eagerly, expectantly.

Gemma pictured the scene in her mind; she also remembered the magazine photo of Paul Verignac in his beach shorts, but resolutely ignored it. She could see herself in the warm atmosphere of the heated pool—and Paul Verignac running his eyes slowly over her figure with a raised eyebrow and a derisive curl to his lips.

'No way,' she said positively. 'You'll have to think of something else.'

'Why not?' Angie asked indignantly. 'It's a great idea.'

'Just because you thought of it, I suppose. Well, I am *not* going to parade myself in a bikini—as near nude as makes no difference—for Paul Verignac's benefit, and that's final. Why, you're as good as asking me to offer myself to him!'

'Of course we're not,' Joy put in. 'That comes later.'

'What did you say?' Gemma turned on her, hardly believing her ears.

Hastily Angie said, 'Don't take any notice of her, Joy was only joking. Look, Gemma, you only have to show yourself to him for a minute, then you can go and change,' she wheedled.

'After all, you ought to let the poor man see what he's getting,' Lisa added, tongue in cheek.

Gemma glared at her and said adamantly, 'No, I refuse to do it, you'll have to think of something else.'

Angie sighed resignedly. 'Oh, all right, then we'll have to fall back on plan B, although the pool idea would have been much easier to arrange, and cheaper too.'

'You mean you'd already thought up an alternative?'

'Well, we thought you might get all prudish, though I don't know why, because your figure isn't that bad.'

Stung, Gemma retorted, 'Men have been known to drool over my figure, let me tell you.'

'So why not let Paul Verignac drool over it?'

Gemma realised she'd fallen neatly into the trap and looked away. 'Because—because he's different,' she answered slowly, then saw them exchanging glances and added hastily, 'You'd better tell me what plan B is.'

Well, it was certainly warm, Gemma had to admit that, but as far as the rest of Angie's alternative plan went she didn't like it one little bit. She was standing in the

centrally heated foyer of a very exclusive Alpine restaurant a few miles outside Zermatt, and was uncomfortably aware of the curious glances she was getting
from the doorman. On arriving there, Gemma had informed him that she was meeting someone and he had
invited her to wait in the bar, looking extremely surprised when she had refused and insisted on waiting in
the foyer near the glass-plated entrance doors, still with
her boots and fur coat on.

The fur was Lisa's, a gorgeous creation in snow lynx
with inset chunky-knit stripes down the front and
sleeves. It also had a hood which Gemma had been instructed to leave down to reveal the wig that Lisa had
spent ages setting into a really elegant swept-up style,
and which made her look extremely sophisticated. Distractedly she undid another button of the coat, nervousness combined with the overheated atmosphere
making her feel hot and tense, her hands clammy. If
their timing was right, Paul Verignac should be driving
up to the restaurant in his car at any moment, and
Gemma strained to keep her eyes on the lamp outside at
the entrance to the car-park; when she saw a torch flash
beside it, it would be time for her to act.

It had taken them three days to set this up; Angie
had been impatient of the delay, but this was the
earliest time they could be absolutely sure of Paul Verignac's movements in the kind of setting they wanted.
Over a dinner table discussion Angie had told them
that she thought they ought to now introduce the air
of mystery more strongly into the experiment. So far,
she reasoned, Gemma could have been just any girl on
a skiing holiday, now they had to make her appear
out of the ordinary and so intrigue Paul Verignac's
curiosity even more. So they had set this up. Their
friend the driver, who was getting fat on Lisa's bribes,
had told them that their victim was meeting a friend

here tonight for dinner and would be arriving alone, driving himself in his car.

At first Angie had wanted Gemma, looking very glamorous, to be dining alone at another table, but she had been talked out of this on the grounds of economy as the restaurant was very expensive, and, as Joy pointed out, if Gemma was going to appear to be that fabulous she'd never have been by herself in the first place. So instead they had hired a fantastic silver-grey Ferrari sports car for a couple of hours, and Gemma was supposed to walk up to it just as Paul Verignac arrived, making quite sure that he saw her get into the car and drive away.

'Why a sports car? Why not a Mercedes or something?' Joy had objected when they had gone along to the garage to choose it.

'Because a sports car is sexy, of course,' Angie explained.

'I don't get it, what's sexy about a chunk of painted metal?'

'Oh, Joy, come on. Can't you picture it?' Lisa asked her, as she let her imagination have full play. 'There'll be Gemma, fabulously dressed in slinky furs, perfectly made-up, a disdainful little pout on her lips, oozing glamour amidst an aura of Chanel No 5. She walks coolly past him as if he didn't exist and then opens the door of this long, low car, a modern-day phallic symbol, sits in it and allows him a glimpse of her long, shapely legs as she swings herself into the seat. Then she drives away into the crisp darkness of the night, leaving him staring after her, wondering who this gorgeous creature is and how he can find her again,' she finished dreamily.

The others were all staring at her, their expressions a display of varied emotions. Joy was impressed. 'Gosh,' she said admiringly, 'I wish I had your imagination, Lisa. I never thought of a car as a phallic symbol before. The M 1 is never going to be the same again!'

Angie, on the other hand, was scathing. 'If that's how your mind works, it's no wonder you wanted to be an actress, you would have been a roaring success—you certainly know how to live the part.'

Gemma didn't say anything; what Lisa had imagined was a nice pipe-dream, but the only part of it that might conceivably come true was where she walked past Paul Verignac as if he didn't exist. In fact, she rather hoped that she'd be able to scuttle past him so fast that he wouldn't even see her!

Now the Ferrari was stationed ready in the restaurant parking area just outside, she could see its bright paintwork gradually becoming hidden under a light covering of snow, the large flakes falling softly past the glass doors and settling into small drifts against the walls of the building. Anxiously she peered out, afraid that she might miss the torch signal. Rather than wait out in the cold, the others were ensconced in a sleigh and were to flash the torch as soon as they saw Paul Verignac turn into the restaurant entrance. They were then to drive to the garage from which they had hired the Ferrari and wait for Gemma to bring it back, afterwards all going on to a party thrown by the Danish crowd, who were going home the next morning.

It all seemed plausible enough, and Gemma was certain that nothing could go wrong this time—for the simple reason that she didn't intend Paul Verignac to even see her. As soon as she saw the signal she intended to put up her hood and make a dash for the car. At least she would be able to tell Angie that they had definitely passed each other, even if it did sound different from what Angie would later write up in her notes. Gemma was getting rather worried about those notes; Angie religiously set aside part of every day to writing up the progress of the experiment and then neatly typing it all out on the portable typewriter she had lugged all the way from England with her—a machine so ancient and noisy that the girls had refused to let her use it in the living-room and banished her to her bedroom while she typed.

Knowing just how inaccurate the progress report was made Gemma frown unhappily, and she was so absorbed in her thoughts that at first she didn't notice the continuous flashes from the gateway; it was only when powerful headlight beams swept into the car-park that she came back to earth with a jolt. Quickly she went to put up her hood, but in her haste and nervousness dropped her evening bag, the contents spilling out over the floor. The doorman came to help her as she stooped to pick them up and jam them back into her bag anyhow, acutely aware that she had only a short time to get outside into the enshrouding darkness where Paul Verignac wouldn't be able to recognise her.

She shut the clasp of her bag with a word of thanks to the doorman and hurried to pull the heavy door open, but he called her back and gave her a lipstick that had rolled away and then insistently came to open the door for her himself, pulling it inwards with maddening slowness and looking at her in open-mouthed surprise as she almost ran past him and out into the open, the hood pulled tightly down and her head bent as if against the snow.

A quick glance showed her that Paul Verignac had parked immediately behind the Ferrari, the two back bumpers only a foot or so apart. He had just finished locking his vehicle and was turning to walk towards the restaurant. Hastily Gemma put up a hand to pull the hood even lower and turned away from him as much as possible. She heard his footsteps crunching on the freezing snow only a few yards away, and then they went on past her. She had left the car unlocked and climbed hastily in, shutting the door behind her with a sigh of relief. She'd done it! At least this time she hadn't fouled everything up for a third time.

Taking the car keys out of her bag, she inserted them in the ignition and started the engine, glancing towards the restaurant as she did so. She could see Paul Verignac silhouetted inside the doorway, being greeted obsequiously by the doorman and helped off with his heavy, fur-collared overcoat. He looked back for a moment, and although Gemma knew it was irrational because he couldn't possible see her properly, she felt a shiver go down her spine and hastily groped for the gear stick, so awkwardly placed by her right hand in this left-hand-drive car, intent on driving away just as fast as she could. Releasing the handbrake, she let out the clutch and put her foot on the sensitive accelerator. The car shot away—not forwards as she had intended, but hard backwards—straight into the back of Paul Verignac's Lamborghini!

There was an appallingly loud crash as metal bit into metal and the unmistakable sound of breaking glass before the engine cut out and there was only silence again. For a moment Gemma was too stunned to move as the full import of what she had done hit her. Oh, no! She put her hands up to her face in an automatic attempt to shut out the world around her, a reflex action from childhood. The temptation to start the car and just drive off, to run away, was almost overwhelming, but then Gemma bit her lip and lifted her chin. The world—or rather Paul Verignac—would just have to be faced. Slowly she started to get out of the car just as he came striding angrily towards her, having heard the noise of the crash from the restaurant.

Yanking her door open wide, he said furiously in French, 'Allow me to tell you, madame, that your

driving is execrable. Perhaps a few lessons might have
been helpful in finding out which gear goes forward
and which in reverse before you actually took control
of a car.'

His tone was infinitely sarcastic, but Gemma ignored
him as she stood up and then went to the back of the
car to see the amount of damage. To her relief it wasn't
as bad as she had expected from the terrible noise of the
collision; her own car had escaped with hardly a
scratch, the over-riders on her rear bumper having
taken the full force of the impact. The Lamborghini,
though, hadn't come off so easily; part of one wing had
been pushed in and all the lights broken on that side.
Gemma was acutely aware of Paul Verignac standing
tall and menacing just behind her, waiting for her to
apologise or something, but she couldn't think of a
thing to say, could only stand with her mind in a whirl,
her face hidden from him by the hood.

'Well, madame?' he asked impatiently.

He still spoke in French and she answered him in
that language. 'Pray accept my apologies, monsieur,' she
managed in a choked voice. 'If—if you will let me know
the cost of the damage I will repay you at once.'

'And just how am I to get in touch with you?'

In her hurry Gemma almost blurted out the phone
number of the chalet, but stopped herself just in time.
If he phoned there and one of the girls answered it, she
could imagine what would happen. They wouldn't
give her any peace until they'd got the whole sorry story
out of her. 'I—I'll telephone you,' she said hastily. 'Tomorrow.' And carefully keeping her back towards him
she started to edge towards the door of her car.

'And just how do you expect to do that if you don't
know my name or where I'm staying?' His tone was
still sarcastic, but there was a definite edge of suspicion
in it now.

'I—I have a pen and paper in my car. I'll get them and you can write your name and address.'

'*Un moment.* That will not be necessary.' He reached into his inside pocket and took out a card, holding it out to her.

Gemma put her hand out to take it, her head still bent, but as she did so, Paul Verignac caught her arm and spun her round.

'Oh!' Her heel slid on the ice, but he caught her, pinning her back against the side of the car. Brusquely he put up his hand and jerked back her hood.

'*Nom d'un nom!* I thought as much. It could only be you!'

He loomed over her, an arm on either side of her so that she couldn't get away, his eyes glaring down at her balefully, flakes of snow falling unheeded on his dark hair. He switched to English as he said harshly, 'There can't be two women in Zermatt who are that stupid and clumsy. Are you always this accident-prone, or are you just some evil spirit who has been sent to punish me in particular? Well, mademoiselle, have you nothing to say for yourself? On the two previous occasions that we have—collided, one can hardly say met—you weren't so reticent.'

Gemma stared up at him. She had heard him, but his words had hardly penetrated. His face was very close to hers, and the tang of his after-shave crept enticingly to her nostrils. He seemed very powerful and masculine. She realised that he was waiting for her to speak and with an effort she pulled herself together sufficiently to say unsteadily, 'The gears were round the wrong way. I—I thought I was in first, but—but it must have been in reverse.' Her voice faded away as she continued to gaze at him.

'Have you ever driven a continental car before?' he demanded.

'N-no.'

'So you get in a powerful car, with which you are completely unfamiliar, and expect to be able to control it in ice and snow and at night, and you don't even know where the gears are!' He stepped away from her and Gemma suddenly found that she could function coherently again. 'You're crazy, do you know that?' Paul Verignac was going on scathingly. 'You would probably have hit every car in the car-park before you got on the road. I take leave to tell you, mademoiselle, that you are nothing but a walking disaster area! If I'd known. . . .'

'Will you please stop yelling at me?' Gemma's raised voice cut him off in mid-flow. 'Anyone would think that I'd absolutely flattened your car! I suppose you're one of those ridiculous men who treat their cars better than they treat their wives and girl-friends. For heaven's sake, it's just a lump of metal, after all.'

'A very expensive lump of metal, mademoiselle. And why not treat it better than a girl-friend; it's much more reliable than any woman,' he added cuttingly. 'More sensitive, and definitely more responsive when handled.'

'Oh!' Gemma's face flamed. 'You're insufferable!' She went to get in her car, but then remembered that she still wasn't supposed to know his name. 'If you'll give me your card, I'll phone you tomorrow to find out the cost of the damage.'

'You're not safe to drive that car anywhere. Where are you going?'

'Mind your own business,' Gemma retorted indignantly.

'Look, I'm not going to be responsible for your smashing into another car and probably killing yourself in the process—not that it wouldn't be a blessing to mankind and me in particular,' he added with heavy sarcasm.

'Why, you....!' Gemma felt white-hot anger rise within her and she took a hasty step towards him, fists clenched.

He caught her wrists before she could raise them and continued to hold them, looking down at her mockingly. 'You were saying, mademoiselle?'

'Let me go!' She struggled futilely to break free until she stood before him, face flushed, panting, knowing that it was useless, that his strength was far greater than hers. 'You chauvinist! I can't stand men who use their physical strength to assert themselves,' she told him accusingly.

'Only because you don't like admitting that we are superior.'

'That's the only thing in which men *are* superior,' Gemma retorted acidly. 'In anything else men are complete nonentities.'

'Are they indeed?' His tone had altered, become silky smooth. 'It seems that you need a few lessons in other aspects of life, besides driving.'

Gemma realised suddenly that she was on dangerous ground. Containing her anger, she said, 'I don't have all night to stand here arguing with you. I'm really quite capable of driving the car. I was—I was just nervous about something before. Please let me go now.'

Slowly he released her wrists, putting up a hand to brush the snow off his hair. 'Very well, mademoiselle, but I insist on making sure of that for myself before I let you venture on the road.'

He held open the door of her car and when she had got in went round to the passenger side and climbed in beside her. His presence so dominated the car that it was impossible to ignore him. Fumblingly she reached out to turn on the ignition.

'Don't you think you ought to make sure it isn't still in gear first?' he asked derisively.

'Of—of course.' Gemma forced herself to sit still for a moment. What on earth was the matter with her? She was acting like an idiot instead of a responsible woman of twenty-two. Just because she'd had an argument with the man didn't mean that she had to go to pieces, did it? Grimly she made herself keep calm while she put the gear lever into neutral and started the engine. Carefully she engaged the gears, making quite sure that it was in first. Remembering how sensitive the accelerator was compared with the cars she was used to, she eased the vehicle slowly forward. There was a slight shudder as it came free from the Lamborghini and then she was driving sedately towards the entrance.

'Twice round the car-park,' Paul Verignac ordered imperatively, sitting sideways so that he could watch her as she drove.

Gemma shot him a fulminating glance, but obeyed. When they had gone twice round without further mishap, she pulled up at one side of the entrance so that he could get out. But he seemed in no hurry to do so, quite unperturbed about keeping his dinner date waiting.

'Well, are you satisfied now?' she asked impatiently.

'So long as you keep driving slowly you should come to no harm,' he conceded. 'What made you nervous earlier?'

'That—that's nothing to do with you,' Gemma answered, lying in her teeth.

'When a girl as beautiful as you gets upset, it usually means that there's a man behind it.'

Eyes wide with surprise at both the implied compliment and his accurate conclusion, Gemma turned her head quickly to look at him. He was watching her intently, the light from the lamp outside emphasising the angles of his face, giving him a lean and predatory appearance. Instinctively she moved a little further away from him and his mouth hardened into a thin line.

She looked away. 'You're mistaken,' she said shortly.

'Am I? I don't think so.' He reached out to cup her chin and turn her face back towards him. His fingers felt strong and cool against the warmth of her skin. 'You haven't yet told me your name?'

'And you haven't given me your card so that I can pay for the damage,' she reminded him, pulling her head away.

He frowned slightly. 'Forget about that, the car's insured. But I would like to....'

'That's very generous of you,' Gemma interrupted him. 'And now could you please get out of my car? I'm meeting some friends and I'm late already.'

Paul Verignac settled his broad shoulders more comfortably, for all the world as if he meant to stay there all night. 'When you've told me your name and where I can get in touch with you,' he replied imperturbably. He put his arm along the back of the seat, his fingers disconcertingly close.

Gemma sat forward. 'Look, if this is some kind of pick-up, forget it. I'm not interested. You're not my type at all.'

'Oh? What is your type, then?' He lifted his hand and with one finger began to trace the curve of her neck.

Jerking her head away, Gemma spun round to face him, moving as far away as possible in the confined limits of the sports car. 'No one as fast as you, that's for sure! And if you don't get out of this car right now I'll put my hand on the horn and hold it there until someone comes,' she threatened, her hand hovering over the button.

To her surprise he laughed. 'Very well, mademoiselle, if you insist. But somehow I have the feeling that it is inevitable that we bump into one another again—I hope not driving our cars next time.' He opened the door and got out, but didn't close it immediately, leaning in to say sardonically, 'By the way, the klaxon on this type of car doesn't work until you turn on the ignition!' With which parting shot he slammed the door and watched until she had driven away, his figure framed in the lamplight.

CHAPTER FOUR

WHEN she arrived at the garage the girls were loud in their demands to know what had kept her, but Gemma fobbed them off while she checked the car in. Hastily she explained what had happened to the mechanic on duty and asked him to phone her the next day if he found any damage. 'Make sure you ask for Miss Kenyon,' she emphasised. He agreed to do so and Gemma ran out to climb into the sleigh with the others, pulling the rug tightly round herself.

'What happened? What took you so long?' Angie asked impatiently.

'He didn't go into the restaurant straightaway,' Gemma told them. 'I had to wait, and then I couldn't resist taking the car for a short drive.' Which was true, because Paul Verignac had insisted on it.

But Gemma didn't enjoy deceiving her friends and was glad that the driver had put the hood up to protect them from the snow so that they couldn't see her face in the darkness.

'Did he get a good look at you? Did he seem at all interested?' Joy was asking eagerly.

'Oh, yes. I think you could say he was definitely intrigued,' she assured them, glad to be able to speak the whole truth for once.

'That's great!' They discussed it excitedly among themselves, occasionally asking Gemma for more details, which she had to swiftly invent, while Lisa helped her to remove the wig and lenses.

The party was being held in a small bar in Zermatt and there were so many of the Danish crowd and their friends that they had virtually taken the place over. Kurt came at once to Gemma, helping her off with her coat and putting a proprietorial arm round her waist as he drew her down beside him on a long wooden seat. Someone gave her a glass of wine, there was music playing, a dish of cheese fondue to dip into, and the atmosphere was warm and friendly. Kurt, too, was very warm and wanted to be even more friendly. Gemma had been out with him several times in the past week —if you can call being in a crowd of at least twelve people going out with someone—and had got on well with him. He was tall and blond and good-looking, although still with the slim figure of a youth, not yet a man. She ought to have been perfectly happy and ready to enjoy herself, but somehow she didn't seem able to enter into the spirit of the thing.

She felt curiously detached, like a spectator instead of a participant. She kept remembering Paul Verignac sitting so close beside her in the car, and when Kurt put his arm across her shoulders and squeezed her, she couldn't help comparing his action with the subtle way Paul had let his fingers caress her neck. Paul! Why, she was even thinking about him by his first name! This just wouldn't do. Determinedly Gemma tried to push all thoughts of him aside and turned to smile at Kurt. He naturally took this as encouragement and leant down to kiss her, which wasn't what she had in mind at all.

By the time the party broke up nearly everyone was in a pleasantly alcoholic haze, although for once Gemma felt quite sober; tonight the wine seemed only to have sharpened her senses. When they came out of the bar it had stopped snowing and a brilliant full moon lit the village almost as clear as day, but silvering the snow that lay so thickly everywhere and softening the scene as the sun could never do. The air felt crisp

and clean, making her senses come alive, the cold biting
into her skin and making it tingle. She took a deep
breath and shivered, pulling the fur hood closer around
her face. The après-ski evenings were beginning to
break up as more people spilled into the village street
from the bars and restaurants, squares of light from the
doors and windows of the quaint Alpine buildings
momentarily breaking the darkness and lighting up the
faces of the passers-by. Horse-drawn sleighs, their bells
ringing merrily, trotted down the centre of the narrow
street, taking people back to their hotels and chalets.
As Gemma stood in the darkened doorway of the bar,
slightly apart from the others, one of the sleighs jingled
by, the matched pair of grey ponies pulling it easily
along. In the back, closely wrapped round by fur rugs,
there were two people, a man and a woman. As they
passed under the nearby lamp, Gemma saw them
clearly. The man was Paul Verignac. The woman with
him was very lovely, a sophisticated platinum blonde
with diamonds flashing at her ears and neck. She clung
to his arm and gazed up at him adoringly, lifting her
hand to pull his head down to kiss her, which he did
lingeringly and passionately, oblivious to everyone
round them.

   The others had begun to move away and Kurt came
to take her hand and join them. 'Gemma, what is it?'
   'What?' She looked at him abstractedly. 'Oh, nothing.' She let him take her hand and lead her along the
street, but looked back over her shoulder, her eyes following the sleigh as it turned into the lane beside the
hotel which she knew led to the chalet that Paul Verignac had taken for the season. Was that woman another
of his conquests, another name for the gossip columnists
to link with his as his latest girl-friend? As she thought
of them together, Gemma felt a surge of emotion that
she was too inexperienced to recognise, but it left her
feeling irritable and unhappy.

Inevitably she wondered what would have happened if she had given Paul Verignac any encouragement earlier that evening; would she have been the one to ride in the sleigh with him, to be kissed so passionately? A little shiver ran down her spine and Kurt pulled her closer, thinking she was cold. Suddenly the fairy-tale element had died out of the night, and Gemma wished she was safely back in England, wished she had never even heard of Paul Verignac.

Twelve hours later the village street was again thronged with holidaymakers, but now the sun was shining brightly and most people were carrying their skis as they made their way to the various slopes and lifts. The four girls had split up this morning; Joy to have a skiing lesson, Lisa to track down her driver friend and find out Paul Verignac's future movements, while Angie remained behind in the chalet to work on her notes. Which left Gemma to buy the wine for their evening meal. There had been some argument before she set out because Angie had insisted she wear the disguise, pointing out that they shouldn't pass up any opportunity for their victim to notice her. Gemma had argued at first, but then capitulated; that Paul had given her another thought was highly unlikely, especially if he had spent the night with that girl—who had obviously been more than willing.

So she went out with the long blonde tresses falling freely to her shoulders and dressed in her own white ski-suit with brown and tan stripes on the sleeves and trousers. At the wine shop she spent half an hour discussing the merits of the various vintages with the friendly proprietor and came out carrying two bottles in a plastic bag. Slowly she sauntered along the street, avoiding the drips of melting snow from the eaves and icicles and gazing in shop windows, the sun warm on her back. Tucked away in a side street she found a little bookshop with an old-fashioned bow-fronted window. She raised her hand to shield her eyes from the sun— and then caught her breath in fascinated wonder.

In the centre of the window, open on a wooden stand, there reposed a book, an ancient handwritten and ornamented manuscript. Gemma pressed her nose close against the panes, trying to decipher the faded writing. Slowly she made out the words, realising that it was a Book of Hours written in mediaeval French. For once she wished she was rich so that she could own such a lovely thing, to be able to read it, touch it, whenever she wanted to instead of only being allowed to look at similar manuscripts in museums and libraries for limited periods under supervision as she had while studying for her degree. For a long time she went on gazing at the beautiful piece of work, wondering what monk had spent so many days and months mixing the paints that he had applied in such meticulous detail over five hundred years ago.

At last she stepped back with an envious sigh, and as she did so a voice almost immediately behind her said, 'What's so fascinating?'

Gemma was so startled that she let go the bag containing the wine, but Paul Verignac's hand shot out and caught it before it hit the ground. 'You!'

'*Mon dieu*, you're as nervous as a cat!' he exclaimed. 'No, mademoiselle, I think it would be safer if I carry these for you,' he added as Gemma reached out to take the bag from him. Instead he took hold of her hand and raised it to his lips, watching her quizzically as he did so. 'You got home safely, then, last night?'

Gemma pulled her hand away in some confusion. 'Yes, of course. Did you?' she added sardonically, remembering the girl.

He raised an eyebrow at her tone. '*Mais oui*.' Looking into the window, he said, 'You haven't yet told me what you found so fascinating. Surely not the manu-script?'

Recalling that he wasn't supposed to like the brainy type, Gemma said hastily, 'Oh, no. That book on the left.'

'*Vraiment?*' His eyebrows rose even higher and he looked distinctly amused.

Puzzled by his reaction, she looked into the window again and to her mortification saw that the book she had indicated was entitled *Lovers through the Ages*, and was open at a page depicting a nude couple in an extremely intimate embrace. She felt herself blushing and turned back to him angrily. 'Not *that* one,' she snapped. But he continued to grin at her maddeningly. 'Will you please give me back my bottles of wine?' she demanded icily.

'No, but I'll carry them for you.' He began to walk back towards the main street and she had no choice but to fall in beside him.

'But you don't know where I'm going,' she objected. 'You might not be heading the same way.'

'I'm going wherever you're going. Why else would I spend the whole morning searching Zermatt for you?'

Stopping dead in her tracks, Gemma stared at him wide-eyed. 'You were looking for me?'

'Of course.' He looked down at her steadily, watching for her reaction, a slight quirk of wry amusement on his lips.

'But why?' Then, because it was the only reason she could think of, she added stiffly, 'If you've changed your mind about the damage to your car, I'm still willing to pay for it.'

To her surprise he looked annoyed. 'Do you really think I would go chasing all over Zermatt to find you to get money from you? You don't know me very well, mademoiselle.'

'I don't know you at all, and I don't *want* to,' Gemma
retorted angrily. 'Will you please give me my wine and
then go away and leave me alone?'

Paul Verignac stared down at her for a moment, his
eyes steely, but then he sighed exasperatedly. 'You
are the most argumentative woman I've ever met. Do
you ever have a conversation lasting for more than two
minutes without starting a fight? Or is it only with me
that the sparks start to fly whenever we meet?'

Gemma gazed up at him for a moment and then
looked quickly down. 'We—we seem to meet in such
unusual circumstances,' she answered rather hollowly.

'We do indeed.' Casually he lifted her chin and
smiled down at her. It was a devastating smile that
must have trapped a dozen women. 'So shall we start
again and take it that I sought you out because you're
one of the most beautiful women I've ever met, and
because I should like to know you much, much better?'
He moved his hand and very gently traced the contour
of her cheek and then the outline of her mouth.

Her heart began to beat painfully loudly and she
found she couldn't answer. She felt completely bowled
over by his experience and charm, his confident assurance that she wouldn't be able to resist him. No one had
ever looked at her like that and called her beautiful before. Her body began to quiver and her lips trembled
beneath his touch; he felt it and a little gleam of
triumph came into his dark, long-lashed eyes. But then
a whole host of things came surging back; the girl he'd
got rid of so brutally a week ago, the woman he had
been with last night, and, most of all, the fact that she
wasn't the person he thought her. If he found her
beautiful it was only because she had made herself into
the type he preferred, the type of woman he wouldn't
let go by without making a pass at.

Gemma lifted her chin and said deliberately, 'That

line is as old as the Alps—and I don't believe a word of it.'

His eyebrows flew up in astonishment, and then, to her surprise, he laughed, a full masculine laugh of genuine amusement. 'You know, mademoiselle, I've a feeling I would have been disappointed if you had said anything else but that. And now, don't you think it's time we introduced ourselves? We can't go on indefinitely addressing each other as monsieur and mademoiselle, can we? My name is Paul Verignac.'

'How do you do.'

'In polite society it is usual to return the compliment,' he reminded her.

Gemma looked at him frowningly. Somehow she felt that the act of telling him her name would alter things between them; at the moment she had all the advantages because she knew everything about him and he nothing whatsoever about her. And up to now she could pretend to herself that the girl he saw wasn't her at all, just the person they'd invented, but once he started addressing her by her name. . . . Slowly she said, 'It's Kenyon. Gemma Kenyon.' And then felt curiously naked, as if she'd revealed her whole identity to him.

But he merely bowed slightly. '*Enchanté*, mademoiselle. A beautiful name for a beautiful woman.' Gemma shot him a darkling glance and he laughed again, holding his hands up in mock surrender and suddenly seeming very French. 'Ah, I forgot. You're English and don't like compliments.'

'Not such obviously fulsome ones as that, anyway,' Gemma retorted. 'And why should being English make me not like compliments?'

He took her arm and led her along the road to where some sleighs were waiting for hire and helped her into one. 'Because Englishmen are so inept at paying compliments and do it so rarely that their women don't know how to receive them, becoming either gauche or suspicious whenever one is paid them,' he told her outrageously as he drew the rug over her knees.

Stung, Gemma instantly leapt to the defence of her countrymen. 'That isn't true at all, and anyway, how would *you* know how an Englishman behaves when he's with a woman?' she asked belligerently.

Paul Verignac gave a slightly crooked grin. 'Shall we say that several Englishwomen have given me reason to believe that they much prefer a Frenchman's approach?' His eyes were filled with mocking amusement and Gemma felt her heart give a strange lurch.

She realised that they were straying on to dangerous ground again and hastily changed the subject. 'Look, just where are we going? The place where I'm staying isn't this way.' The sleigh was bowling along towards the outskirts of the village in the opposite direction to the chalet.

'I thought you might like to see the ice-skating races at the lake. You don't have to get back yet, do you?'

'Well, no, I suppose not,' Gemma admitted, but resentful of his high-handed manner, added, 'But what makes you think I want to go anywhere with you?'

'It's purely a matter of self-preservation. We were bound to collide some time during the day and I think it will be safer if I keep an eye on you—at least then I'll have some chance of averting a catastrophe.'

Gemma laughed. 'Now *that* I do believe!' She looked at him, eyes alight with mischief, the sun turning the blonde hair to molten gold.

For a second his expression altered, became serious, but was quickly replaced by his usual slightly sardonic smile.

There was already a crowd round the lake watching the first of the ice-skating championship races, but Paul used his shoulders to find a vantage point for

THE ICE MAIDEN

them. The races were an important event because the winner would almost certainly be picked to represent his country in the next winter Olympics, so there was great excitement as the contestants lined up for the various heats.

'Which one do you think will win?' Paul asked idly.

Gemma looked at the line of men in their tight-fitting suits and gaily-coloured safety helmets with a considering air. 'That one. The third from the left in the red helmet.'

'You sound very definite.'

They watched the race closely as the men lapped the marked out circuit on the deeply frozen lake, the one Gemma had picked out coming first by several yards.

'Did you know who he was?' Paul asked in some astonishment.

'No.' Gemma gave a little shrug. 'I'm just lucky with things like that.'

'See if you can pick out the one for the next race.'

Almost casually she ran her eyes over the competitors and then pointed. 'The one almost in the middle. Number twenty-one.'

'Ah, yes, I see him.' Paul looked at her quizzically. 'Would you care to have a bet on it?'

'No, thanks. I don't gamble.'

The glance he gave her was rather sceptical, but he didn't press the point. Number twenty-one came in an easy winner and over the next four races Gemma picked the winner in all but the final; for this she couldn't make up her mind between two men, and in the event the race was so close that they had to wait for an announcement before they knew that one of those she'd picked had won.

Paul was incredulous. 'How on earth did you do it?'

Shrugging, Gemma said, 'I told you, I'm just lucky.'

'Perhaps there's something about the person who's

going to win—an air of determination or something that you instinctively recognise?' he conjectured.

'Possibly, but I'm lucky with other kinds of contests —picking out numbers, that kind of thing.'

'Numbers?' He was looking at her intently now. 'Are you also lucky at games of chance—roulette, for instance?'

'I don't know, I've never played it.'

'Well, you're going to have the chance to find out. There's a casino in the hotel where I'm staying. We'll go there tonight and see if your luck extends to the gaming tables.'

He had taken hold of her arm, just below the elbow, but Gemma pulled away. 'No, thanks,' she said shortly, and went to walk away from him.

In two strides he caught up with her and turned her round to face him. 'Why not? Are you afraid?'

'I told you, I don't gamble. Gambling is for people who are too jaded to get their kicks any other way,' she told him bluntly. 'If that's what turns you on, okay, but leave me out of it.'

'Most people who take that attitude do so only because they're afraid of losing,' he answered scathingly.

Gemma flushed angrily. Bitingly she retorted, 'Possibly because they know they can't *afford* to lose.'

Looking at her angry face, Paul said soothingly, '*Doucement, ma petite.* I only wanted to see if this extraordinary talent you have extends to other things. I'll supply the stake money. Win or lose, you don't have to worry.'

'And why should I put myself out to line your pockets even further?' She was still angry, still resentful.

Impatiently he said, 'I told you, I just want to see if you can do it. If we win we'll give the money to charity. Will you do it on those terms?'

'Any charity I like?' Gemma asked suspiciously.

'Any charity you like,' he agreed, an eager light in his eyes as he saw that he was winning her round.

Gemma took a deep breath. 'All right, on those terms I'll do it.'

He took her to lunch in a small, intimate restaurant and wanted her to spend the rest of the afternoon with him, but Gemma steadfastly refused. A couple of hours in his disturbing company was more than enough, and she still had to try to think of some way of persuading the girls to let her go out alone tonight, and in her disguise. But things worked out far more easily than she expected.

When she got back to the chalet, clutching her bottles, she found only Lisa and Angie there, both of them looking rather despondent.

'Hi. Where's Joy?' she asked them.

'Still out on the slopes. I think she's taken a yen to that Italian ski-instructor,' Lisa told her. 'Where have you been?'

'Oh, window-shopping, and then I went to watch the ice-skating at the lake.' Gemma unpacked the bottles of wine and put them in the fridge, then dropped into an armchair while she pulled off her boots. 'You look pretty glum, what's the matter?'

Angie and Lisa looked at one another and then Angie said slowly, 'We've had a setback concerning the experiment. Unfortunately there's been an unforeseeable hitch. We'll probably have to call the whole thing off, but I don't suppose you'll be too disappointed,' she added gloomily.

'What hitch?'

It was Lisa who answered. 'When I went to talk to Paul Verignac's driver today, he told me that an old girl-friend of Verignac's had arrived in Zermatt—a Frenchwoman called Louise Julien. Apparently they had a pretty hot affair a couple of years ago, but then they had a row and she married some terrifically rich industrialist on the rebound. But now she's left her husband and come running back to Paul Verignac. It was she he had dinner with last night and he took her back to his chalet.'

'So the chances of him falling for you when he's heavily involved with his ex-girl-friend are rather remote,' Angie said caustically. 'Oh, it's such a shame! All that time and effort wasted, not to speak of all the money we've spent on coming here—especially Lisa.' She threw down the pen she was holding and sat back moodily in her chair.

So that was who the woman was she had seen him with. Gemma frowned abstractedly. So where had the woman been this morning? Could it be that they had had another row, or had Paul just let her stay the night —perhaps slept with her—and then kicked her out in the morning?

'You haven't said anything, Gemma. What do you think, should we call the whole thing off? After all, you're the one who's most deeply involved.'

Gemma stood up and came over to them. 'No, I'm quite sure we shouldn't. I don't know what he's done with Louise Julien, but I saw Paul Verignac this morning and she certainly wasn't with him then.'

'You saw him? Where?' Angie's gloom dropped away like a discarded coat.

'In Zermatt, while I was shopping.'

'Did he see you?' Lisa asked eagerly. 'Thank goodness she was wearing the wig,' she added to Angie.

Gemma paused while they both looked at her expectantly. 'Yes,' she admitted. 'He did see me. And as a matter of fact he—he said good morning.'

'That's marvellous!' Angie came to her feet and hugged her excitedly. 'Now we really can go ahead—

and when I thought the whole thing was over too. I'll get my notes and start work straightaway.' She almost ran out of the room to hurry up to her bedroom where she kept the computer print-out.

Lisa was looking at Gemma curiously. 'For someone who's been against this whole experiment from the start, you just behaved very strangely, Gemma, my girl. Why this sudden change of attitude? I thought that you, more than any of us, would have been more than willing to chuck the whole thing in, but instead of that you're urging us to go ahead. Why, Gemma?'

'For the reasons that Angie said, of course. We've already spent a lot of time and energy on the experiment and it would be a shame if we couldn't finish it.' Gemma lifted her arms to take off the wig, obscuring her face.

But Lisa wasn't to be put off so easily. 'It wouldn't be because you've fallen for Paul Verignac, would it?' she asked suspiciously.

'Of course not! I've hardly spoken to the man.' Gemma took off the wig and shook her hair free, managing to speak with just the right degree of asperity. In fact, she didn't know herself why she'd made it possible for them to go on. It would have been so simple just to agree with the others, and it would have been a relief not to have to dress up in this ridiculous wig any more and to pretend that she was something she wasn't. She should have been glad that the opportunity had presented itself to stop deceiving her friends and let the whole thing die—so why hadn't she grabbed it with both hands?

Crossing to a chair, Gemma picked up a magazine and pretended to read it, aware that Lisa was still watching her closely. She tried to tell herself that she was only going on for the sake of the others and the work they'd put into the experiment, that the reasons for not letting them down still applied. But at length she had to admit the truth; that she had never known a man like Paul Verignac before and that his dominant masculinity had aroused something in her that no other man had ever evoked. His air of sardonic amusement seemed to act as a challenge to her. He was so sure of himself and his ability to dominate her sex, to pick them up or drop them as he willed, that she felt an irresistible urge to fight him, to show him that there was one woman at least who was impervious to his charm. And by telling the others that they could go on with the experiment she had symbolically picked up the gauntlet; there was no going back now. A sudden feeling of intense excitement filled her; Paul Verignac thought he could use women as he wanted, going from one to another as casually as the bee goes from flower to flower; it would be very interesting to see his face when he finally found out that he in turn had been used and discarded.

Angie came clattering back into the room and dropped the print-out on the table with a thud. 'Do you realise we have less than a month of our vacation left? If we're going to get Gemma engaged to Paul Verignac we'll have to work fast, and this is the most crucial point of the whole thing—how to get Gemma into a position where he can meet her. Have either of you any ideas?'

Cautiously Gemma waited for Lisa to speak first. 'Well, as he's already spoken to Gemma we're half way there. All we have to do is stand her where he can't miss her and leave the rest to him. Somehow I can't see Paul Verignac passing up an opportunity like that,' Lisa added wryly. 'After all, we've almost thrown Gemma at his head for the past week.'

'He usually has dinner at his hotel, doesn't he?' Gemma asked casually.

Lisa nodded. 'Why, what have you in mind?'

'Well, as we've so little time left, I thought that perhaps I could go to his hotel tonight and take a chance on seeing him. I could wait in the bar until he came out of the restaurant, or something.'

If anything the suspicious frown on Lisa's expressive face deepened, but she refrained from saying anything. Angie, however, was full of enthusiasm for the suggestion. 'That's a good idea, Gemma. Although,' she paused, 'we don't want it to look as if you're hanging around to pick somebody up. It wouldn't do for him to get that impression.'

'Oh, I shouldn't worry,' Lisa broke in. 'I'm sure Gemma will be able to handle the situation so that it looks like a casual meeting. Won't you, Gemma?' she added pointedly.

Refusing to be drawn, Gemma answered composedly, 'I'll try, of course. But if you don't like the idea we can always think of something else. I only suggested it because you said we were running out of time.'

'No, it sounds fine to me, if you don't mind doing it, Gemma?'

Avoiding Lisa's eyes, Gemma replied coolly, 'Not if it helps the experiment.'

So when Joy got back to the chalet later she found the three of them busily preparing; Lisa was setting the spare wig into a new style, Angie was letting down the hem of one of Lisa's best evening dresses, while Gemma herself was painting her nails under Lisa's supervision.

'Hey, what's going on?'

'Where have you been?' Angie demanded. 'Don't sit down, I want you to get on the phone to the horse-taxi company and tell them to send a sleigh up here to collect Gemma at seven-thirty.'

'Why, where's she going?' Joy looked at them expectantly, but they were all too intent on what they were doing to answer. 'Will somebody tell me what's happening?' she complained.

'Everything's on again. Gemma's going down to the hotel to try to meet Paul Verignac tonight,' Angie explained.

'Wow!' Joy made the phone call and enthusiastically came to help.

By the time the sleigh arrived they had dressed Gemma up in Lisa's dress, a beautifully cut midnight-blue swathed sheath that clung in all the right places without detracting from its femininity. The wig Lisa had set into large curls on the crown with the back and sides falling into a heavy bell around her face.

'The hairclips holding the wig on won't show, will they?' Joy asked anxiously.

'No, that's why I put the big curls on top. If he does see a clip he'll think it's just to hold the curls in place,' Lisa explained. She looked at Gemma critically, surveying her handiwork with some pride. As it was the evening she had used more eye make-up, applying two shades of blue eye-shadow to make Gemma's eyes look larger and to emphasise the deep blue of the lenses, already heightened by the complementary colour of the dress.

'She could do with some jewellery,' Angie pointed out. 'A necklace or something.'

None of them, however, possessed anything suitable until Joy produced a brooch in the shape of a scorpion with a sharply pointed tail.

'I like the idea of that,' Gemma laughed. 'It's very apt.'

'Just so long as Paul Verignac doesn't find out he's being stung,' Lisa warned. 'Be careful, Gemma, if he realises what you're doing he might turn nasty.'

They looked at one another, their excitement suddenly sobered, perhaps for the first time realising that they could be playing with fire.

'Don't worry, I'll be all right,' Gemma assured them with an optimism that didn't ring true. 'Keep your fingers crossed for me.'

She put on Lisa's fur coat again and they saw her into the sleigh, waving until she was out of sight. Automatically Gemma pulled the fur rugs closer around her to keep out the cold, but strangely she didn't feel cold at all, her pulses raced and she was filled by a confused mixture of anticipation and apprehension. The sleigh moved swiftly through the streets and the brightly lit entrance to the hotel came in sight much too soon. She gulped and almost called out to the driver to stop and take her back to the chalet, but then the moment passed. As they pulled up under the covered entrance way and the doorman hurried to help her out, Gemma took a deep breath and then deliberately walked into the hotel and back into the masquerade.

He was waiting for her in the foyer, looking even taller and more powerful in an immaculate black evening suit, the crisp whiteness of his frilled shirt emphasising a tan gained on the ski slopes. He watched her as she came in, making no immediate move to greet her, leaning his broad shoulders against a magazine booth, a cigarette between his fingers. Gemma stopped a few yards away from him and waited for him to come to her. He drew on the cigarette and then slowly ground it out in an ashtray, taking his time about it, before walking across to her, a crooked grin on his mouth.

'I ought to be very cross with you, you're late.' He took her hand to raise it to his lips.

Gemma immediately snatched it back. 'I can always go away again,' she informed him tartly. Was he so used to women running after him that he couldn't even wait a quarter of an hour for one?

His eyebrows flew up at her outburst. 'You're pricklier than a hedgehog!'

Gemma bit her lip. 'I'm sorry. I couldn't avoid it, I

was delayed,' She had tried to get the others to order a sleigh earlier, but they had said that Paul wouldn't possibly have dinner before then, and she had been afraid she might arouse Lisa's suspicions even further if she insisted.

'Let me help you with your coat.' He gave the fur to an attendant and ran his eyes over her appreciatively. 'If I didn't know that you disliked flattery so much, I would tell you how lovely you look. Your dark brows and lashes against your blonde hair make a stunning combination.'

Gemma looked up at him, laughing inwardly; if he only knew just how false the compliment was! But she merely smiled at him and said, *'Merci du compliment, monsieur.'*

'You're learning fast.' Taking her arm, he led her into the dining-room where the maître d'hotel hurried forward to show them to a table set discreetly in an alcove. Many people looked at them as they passed, some curiously, some, both men and women, in open admiration or envy. For they made a good-looking couple; Gemma caught a glimpse of them both in a mirrored pillar and was surprised into realising it. She smiled rather cynically, wondering if Cinderella had felt the same when she met the Prince at the ball. Well, at least Gemma ad the advantage of being able to stay out later than idnight before she turned back into her ordinary self again.

'You should have let me call to collect you. Where exactly are you staying?' he asked her when they were seated.

'In a chalet on the outskirts of the village.'

'A house-party chalet, belonging to a tour operator?' The waiter handed them the menus. 'Would you like an aperitif?'

'A dry Martini, please.'

Paul gave the order and Gemma lifted the menu to study it, but he pulled it down so that he could see her face. 'You didn't answer my question,' he reminded her, his dark eyes watching her closely.

'What? Oh, no, it isn't a house-party, it's a private chalet.'

'And you're staying there with your family?'

'No, with friends.' Hastily she changed the subject. 'This is a fabulous hotel. I hear it has an Olympic-sized swimming pool?'

If he noticed her ploy, he let it pass, but several times during the course of the meal he tried to bring the conversation back to her, attempting to find out about her. Gemma told him as little as she possibly could, saying casually that her family lived in Norfolk, but keeping quiet about Oxford, letting him get the impression that she was supported by her parents and didn't have to work. He, in turn, told her something of his business interests, which seemed to take up very little of his life, and she gathered that he spent most of his time jet-setting wherever the fancy took him. This was so much the picture of him shown up by the computer that for a moment Gemma was unable to keep the contempt she felt for his way of life out of her eyes.

She covered the slip quickly, hastily lowering her head, but his hand came over hers and gripped it cruelly. Gemma gave a little wince of pain.

'Do you find my life-style so disgusting?' His voice was harsh and he hadn't loosened the grip on her hand any.

'N-no, of course not.' Gemma tried not to let him see that he was hurting her. 'It—it just seemed rather pointless, that's all.'

His lips twisted cynically. 'And does yours have any more point to it?'

For a moment her eyes flashed at him and she was

on the point of telling him of her ambitions for the
future when she'd got her M.A., but she remembered in
time and merely said, 'No, I suppose not. I'm sorry,
you have every right to live your life the way you
want.'

He glared at her, but she returned his gaze steadily
until he looked away, a brooding look on his face.
Loosening his hold on her hand, he swirled the brandy
in his glass and then drank it down in one swallow.

'If you've finished we might as well go through to the
gaming-tables.'

The Casino was on the first floor of the hotel, a large
high-ceilinged room already quite full of well-dressed
people who clustered round the various tables or stood
in laughing, chattering groups. Paul took some gambling chips from his pocket and handed them to her,
but Gemma hung back.

'I don't know how to play. You'd better show me
first.'

'*Eh bien.*' He led the way to one of the roulette tables
and sat down in a vacant chair, Gemma standing behind him so that she could watch. Most of the people
round the table were talking to their neighbours while
they played, but some of them had an intent look on
their faces, their eyes never leaving the ball as it spun
round the wheel. Paul placed two of his chips on one
of the black numbers but didn't win, and the croupier
raked in the bet.

After about a quarter of an hour in which he lost
consistently, Paul turned to her. 'Do you think you have
the hang of it now?' He was smiling again, his earlier
anger gone—but not, Gemma thought, forgotten.

She nodded. 'Yes, it seems quite easy.'

He got up and surrendered his place to her. Gemma
picked up one of the chips and almost dropped it again
when she saw how much it was worth. Even allowing

for the number of francs to the pound, it was a lot of
money, she realised as she did some rapid mental arith-
metic. She searched among the chips for some of a
smaller value, but there weren't any. Turning her
head, she looked up at Paul questioningly. He gave a
slight nod and indicated that she should play.

Gemma gave a gulp and picked up a chip, looking at
the numbers carefully before she put it on red twenty-
two. It lost, but the second time her number came up
and the croupier pushed a little pile of chips towards
her. The success gave her confidence as she went on
playing. She by no means won every time, but she
won more often than she lost and she began to become
intent on the game, concentrating on the gyrations of
the ball as closely as the others. The pile of chips beside her was growing steadily and soon people realised
that she was having a run of luck and followed her bets
so that the house began to lose quite heavily. There
was a feeling of tense expectancy around the table now
every time she decided on a number, as everyone waited
to place their chips on the same square.

Thoroughly lost in the game, Gemma picked up a
small pile of chips, deliberating which number to
choose. Paul had been standing behind her chair all the
while, making no attempt to influence her judgment
in any way, but perhaps the tenseness had got to him
too, because now he put his hands down to grip her
shoulders, his fingers pressing into her shoulder blades.
Gemma hesitated, and then dropped the chips on one
of the squares. It lost and there was a groan from round
the table. She found that her concentration had gone
and the next two squares she picked almost at random.
They lost again, and several of the players looked at her
resentfully, as though it was her fault they had lost
their money.

Paul leaned down and said quietly, 'I think you've

played enough for tonight. Shall we go and have a drink?'

Gemma stood up in some relief and watched as Paul picked up the piles of chips, first tossing some to the croupier. He changed them at the desk and put an impressive roll of notes into his pocket, then he put his arm round her waist and led her out of the Casino into a lounge where a small band played softly for the few couples who were dancing.

He pulled out a chair for her. 'I think this calls for champagne, don't you?' And when it came he lifted his glass to her. 'Congratulations. You did remarkably well.'

Gemma laughed rather nervously. 'I thought I was going to lose it all again.'

'What made your luck change, I wonder?'

'I don't know.' Reaction had begun to set in after the tension of the game and she suddenly felt very tired, leaning back in her chair and sipping the champagne, savouring the coolness of the drink, her eyes half closed.

'Would you like to dance?'

Gemma opened her eyes to find Paul watching her. He had a cigarette between his fingers, but there was a long head of ash on it, as though he had forgotten to smoke it. Their eyes met and held. His expression didn't alter, but Gemma suddenly found that she was trembling. Deliberately she raised her glass and drained it. 'Why not?' There was the slightest trace of defiance in her voice.

The small dance floor wasn't very crowded, it was late and most people went out to the livelier bars in the evenings. Paul took her in his arms, drawing her against him. For a moment she resisted, strangely unwilling to be held so intimately close, but then gave a mental shrug and relaxed, one hand on his shoulder, the other he held against his chest. Why she felt reluctant she couldn't explain; she had danced even closer than this with Kurt only last night, and with countless others over the years, but somehow it was different with Paul. She glanced up at him and surprised a speculative look in his eyes which was quickly hidden.

'Don't you want to know how much money you've won?' he asked.

'I didn't think you'd worked it out yet.'

'I did a rough count when I changed the chips. It's about three thousand.'

'Three thousand francs? As much as that?' Gemma gazed at him in awe.

'No, three thousand pounds.' He watched her narrowly, a thin smile on his lips.

Gemma's footsteps faltered and he pulled her closer to prevent her stumbling. 'But—but that's a fortune! I'd no idea it was so much.'

Softly he said, 'And it's all yours.'

For a moment Gemma let the thought of all that lovely money fill her mind. Three thousand pounds! No, it was so much that it was unimaginable. She realised that Paul again had a speculative look in his eyes. Frowning slightly, she said, 'What do you mean, it's all mine? We agreed that we would give any winnings to charity.'

'Charity begins at home; isn't that one of your English sayings?'

Her voice hardened. 'Do you mean that you want to keep the money?'

'No, as I said, it's yours. I'm sure you could find a use for it—extend your holiday, or buy a new fur coat perhaps.'

Gemma came to a stop and pulled away from him. 'Just what kind of person do you think I am? I said I'd give the money to charity and I meant it.' She glared up at him angrily.

'So what are we arguing about?'

He drew her against him again, the speculative look replaced by one of wry amusement, but Gemma held herself stiffly, still angry at his assumption that she was mercenary, so when he said, 'May I see you again tomorrow?' she was taken completely by surprise.

Her eyes flew up to look at him, but she could read nothing from his expression, his face gave nothing away. 'Why, so we can play at roulette again?' she asked tartly.

'Not unless you particularly want to,' he replied equably.

'I don't.'

'Then we will do something else. How would you like to ski down into Italy?'

Surprised, she asked, 'Can you do that?'

'Yes, you take the lifts up to Theodulpass or Furggsattel just below the Matterhorn and then ski all the way down to Cervinia in Italy. You can either do the return journey in reverse or come back by sleigh.'

'That sounds wonderful. I'd love to do it,' she exclaimed.

'Good, then I'll come and pick you up tomorrow at nine-thirty. Don't forget to bring your passport.'

'Oh, but I didn't mean that I'd....' Gemma looked up at him helplessly. She wasn't at all sure that she wanted to spend tomorrow with the enigmatic Paul Verignac, but it seemed she was going to.

'What's the address of your chalet?' he was asking.

'Er—it would be out of your way to come there. I'll meet you in the village square at ten,' she told him, carefully avoiding his eyes that seemed to see far too much.

'It's no bother.'

'No, I'd rather meet you in the square.'

She felt him give a slight shrug. '*Eh bien*. Then that's settled.'

The band changed tempo to a smoochy number and the lights dimmed, only coloured spotlights reflecting off a revolving central mirrored ball hanging from the ceiling sending weird patterns over the walls and the dancers. Paul let go of her hand and moved his own low down on her hips, holding her close to him. She felt his body, taut and masculine against her own. For a second a glancing spotlight lit his face, his mouth sensuous, his eyes intent, before he lowered his head and sought her lips. His mouth was hard and firm against hers, demandingly urgent, and for a surprised few moments she responded to that demand, but then realisation of where they were came flooding back and she became rigid beneath his hands, trying to turn her head away. He wouldn't let her at first and she had to struggle against him before he finally lifted his head.

'How dare you?' she hissed at him angrily. 'Let me go at once!'

'What's the matter?' he asked jeeringly. 'Don't you like being kissed?'

'I certainly don't like being pawed in public. Now will you please let go of me?'

'All right.' He went to move away from her, but didn't get very far.

'I told you to let me go,' Gemma commanded, getting really angry now.

His voice was dry. 'I would be happy to oblige you, Gemma, but that brooch thing you're wearing appears to have got caught on the pocket of my jacket.'

'Oh.' Gemma squinted down and tentatively tried to pull away from him, but found that the points of the scorpion's tail were firmly embedded into the material of his pocket.

'You'll have to undo the brooch,' he advised her.

Putting her hands up between them, her face flushed as much with embarrassment as anger, she tried to free the brooch, but it had a complicated safety catch and she couldn't manage it. 'I can't do it,' she hissed at him. 'You'll have to try.'

'Very well.' He put his hands up, while Gemma blushed furiously, uncomfortably aware that people had begun to watch them and how it would appear. To add to her discomfort the band came to the end of their number.

'The band's stopped. We can't stand here. What are we going to do?' she asked in a panic.

'We shall just have to pretend that we can't bear to let each other go.' Paul put his arm round her and they moved off the floor in a sort of crabwise walk, their chests close together. His voice sounded strange and when Gemma looked at him she found to her fury that he was choking with suppressed laughter.

'It is *not* funny!'

They reached the corridor where they received several startled looks from people waiting for the near-by lifts before Paul steered her into the comparative privacy of an empty games room. And here he gave way to his mirth while Gemma grew more irate.

'Don't just stand there laughing, you big fool! Take your jacket off and let me try to get the brooch free.'

Still grinning, he took off his coat and held it while she tried, unsuccessfully to get the brooch off. 'It's no good,' she said with a groan. 'It won't come off without tearing the material.'

'Well, I'm afraid I shall need my jacket when I go back to my chalet, so there's only one thing to do.' He reached into his trousers pocket and took out a small penknife, flicking it open and advancing on her with the blade.

Gemma almost had a heart attack as she thought he was about to cut her dress to free the brooch. She had a vision of Lisa's face when she saw it and cried out, 'No! You mustn't cut the dress.'

'I don't intend to.' ...... the blade and skilfully cut round the stitches so that ... pocket came away from the jacket and she was left with only the small square of material hanging on the brooch.

Unhappily she looked at him. 'Thank you. I hate to say it, but I'm afraid your jacket's ruined.'

He shrugged. 'Not necessarily. I can probably have another one put on. It's nothing.'

'Well, I'm not going to offer to pay for it this time. It was entirely your own fault.'

'For kissing you when there were other people around? Why should you care what people think?'

Gemma flushed and said shortly. 'Well, I do, that's all.'

'A very bourgeois attitude,' he said sneeringly.

'Bourgeois or not, that's how I feel.' She went to walk past him out of the room, but he put an arm against the wall and stopped her.

'Where are you going?'

'Home, of course.'

'Won't you come back to my chalet for a night-cap first?'

'No—thank you.'

Ducking beneath his arm, Gemma almost ran out of the room into the foyer. She had to wait a few minutes for her coat and he came leisurely up to hold it for her.

'Haven't you forgotten your winnings?'

He took out the roll of notes and held them out to her. For a moment she hesitated, then took them from him. His lips twisted into a thin smile of sardonic amusement.

Reeling off a hundred franc-note, Gemma said caustically, 'This is for my taxi fare.' Then she walked across to the reception desk where there was a collection box for Swiss orphans. The receptionist's eyebrows nearly disappeared into his hairline as Gemma stuffed the

wad of notes into it. She ▮▮▮▮ to find Paul watching
her with an arrested expression on his face. 'Good
night, Monsieur Verignac,' she said evenly. 'It's been
an interesting evening.'

Turning, she walked through the door that an aston-
ished doorman was holding open for her and climbed
into a waiting sleigh. Before it could move off Paul
came quickly up to her, the sarcasm completely gone
as he said, 'I never thought you'd really do it.' Then, '*A
demain*. Until tomorrow. Ten o'clock in the square.'

'Don't bother. You'll be wasting your time.'

Without warning he caught her hand and raised it to
his lips, turning it so that he pressed the kiss into her
palm. When she didn't draw back he smiled, his mouth
cynical again. 'You'll be there.' He stepped back and
raised his hand in casual farewell as the sleigh pulled
away.

CHAPTER FIVE

GEMMA found that she was sitting tensely upright, her fingers gripping her evening bag tightly. Slowly she forced herself to relax and lean back against the seat, but rage still throbbed through her veins. How dared he treat her like some cheap little money-grabber? Expecting her to keep the money, kissing her when people were watching? She was so hot with anger that she hardly felt the cold as the sleigh trotted through the streets, its lamps lighting the way as the moon slid behind a cloud. Remembering that his pocket was still attached to her brooch, she gingerly pulled at the square of material until it tore free. As she looked at it, her anger gradually subsided; she supposed that getting caught up like that had been funny when she really thought about it. As her fingers smoothed the piece of fabric her mouth twisted into a reluctant grin and she wondered why she hadn't seen the funny side of it at the time.

Her brows drew into a frown as the smile faded; because she had been too enraged by his kiss to even think about anything else, that was why. And she shouldn't have been. No way should a simple kiss have so affected her. A dozen boy-friends must have kissed her in public, and in broad daylight too, let alone in the semi-darkness of a dimly lit dance floor, and although she might have objected she had never reacted so violently before. For her reaction had been violent and, she had to admit, out of all proportion to the offence. So why had it so enraged her, made her want to get right away from Paul as quickly as possible?

As she thought about it the solution gradually came to her. Because Paul Verignac had kissed her as no other man had ever done before; the experience gained from encounters with a hundred other women had shown in the way he had held her against him, letting her feel his need of her, his lips strong with the masculine demand for submission. Colour flooded into Gemma's cheeks. His expertise and urgency had startled and frightened her. And he had had so many women. To him she was just another name to add to the list, a source of amusement until she gave him what he wanted, then to be discarded in search of other prey. Lifting her hand, she wiped her mouth, trying to rid herself of his touch, but even as she did so her hand was trembling.

The girls were still up when she got back to the chalet, eagerly waiting to find out what had happened.

'It's no good you asking questions, I'm not going to tell you a thing until I've changed,' she insisted as they came crowding to meet her.

Lisa, who was always more perceptive than the others, saw the tenseness round her eyes and came upstairs with her to run a bath and help her undress. Then she left her alone while Gemma creamed off her make-up; without it she looked younger than her twenty-two years and infinitely more vulnerable. She knew that the others were waiting for her, agog with curiosity, but somehow she hadn't the energy to hurry. It felt good to lie back in the bath and let the tensions ebb away, her skin caressed by the warm water, her nostrils enjoying the scent of her herbal bath oil. Extravagantly she had poured in all that was left in the bottle. Never mind, she could get some more tomorrow, she thought dreamily. But tomorrow Paul would be waiting for her in the village square, might even come looking for her if she didn't turn up. Her fingers tightened convulsively on her sponge, and then she got out of the bath and began to dry herself rapidly. Even in his absence, Paul Verignac's personality was too dominant to be pushed aside.

'Well?' Angie demanded as soon as she came downstairs, her dressing-gown wrapped warmly round the thin cotton of her pyjamas. 'What happened? You did meet him, didn't you?'

'Yes, I met him all right.' Gemma gratefully accepted a mug of steaming cocoa from Lisa and sat in the armchair by the fire, tucking her feet under her.

'What was he like? Was he as gorgeous as his photograph?' Joy wanted to know as she came to sit on the floor at Gemma's feet, looking up at her avidly.

Gemma thought about it. 'Even more so, I should think,' she answered slowly. 'He's certainly extremely good-looking, and he has great charm—when he wants to use it,' she added drily.

'Meaning that he did or he didn't, with you?' Lisa asked as they all stared at her.

Gemma shrugged. 'Both, I suppose.'

Impatiently Angie interrupted, her orderly mind not liking the way things were going. 'Start at the beginning, Gemma, tell us how you managed to meet him.' She held her pen poised ready over her notebook.

'I didn't have to do anything, he came up and started talking to me.' Which was at least half true. 'He asked me to have dinner with him and afterwards he took me to the Casino in the hotel and we played roulette,' she added matter-of-factly, enjoying the rather stunned looks on their faces.

Awed, Joy said, 'You make it sound so commonplace. Almost as if you frequented gambling hells every day of the week.'

'It was hardly a gambling hell,' Gemma protested. 'It was all very respectable and quite dull really. You just sat around a table and put money on numbers and they either came up or they didn't.'

'Whose money did you play with?' Angie demanded practically.

'His. He showed me how to play and then he staked me.'

'How much did you win?' Lisa wanted to know. They were all used to her uncanny knack of picking winners and it never occurred to them that she might lose.

Gemma looked round at them slowly, not loath to let the suspense build up a little. Distinctly she said, 'Three thousand pounds.'

They gaped at her and Joy let out a long breath. 'Gemma, that's a fortune! Did he give you any of it?' she asked anxiously.

'All of it. He said it was all mine.' Gemma's face tightened as she remembered.

'You mean he gave you three thousand pounds?' Angie's voice was a breathless squeak. 'My God, we're rich!' She sat back and stared at Gemma, her notepad forgotten.

'So where is it?' Lisa was eyeing her taut face closely.

Gemma looked down at her mug intently. 'I haven't got it any more. I put it all in a collecting box for orphans,' she told them baldly.

There was a dumbfounded silence until Joy said hollowly, 'All of it? You didn't keep any of it?'

'Only a hundred francs, and I gave that to the sleigh-driver.'

'Why, Gemma?' Lisa asked quietly.

Raising her head, Gemma looked at them steadily. 'Because I don't approve of gambling, you know that.'

'But that wasn't the only reason, was it?' Lisa pursued.

Surprised by the tone of her voice, Joy and Angie

looked at her quickly, then back at Gemma.

'No,' she admitted. A slight note of defiance entered her voice as she said, 'He—he made me angry. I'd
already said that any winnings would go to charity,
but he seemed to take it for granted that I'd go back
on my word when I knew it was such a large amount.
It almost seemed as if he wanted me to be the gold-
digging type. And then he....' She stopped abruptly.

'Go on, Gemma, you can't leave it there,' Angie said
urgently.

'No, I suppose not.' Gemma drained her cocoa and
set the mug down on the floor. She shrugged and said
tightly, 'We were dancing. He started to get fresh and
I told him what I thought of it. Then I left.'

'After you'd put the money in the collecting box?'
Joy asked.

'Yes.'

'That's it, then.' Angie sat back disconsolately. 'I
was beginning to think that giving the money away
was the best thing you could have done—it would certainly have intrigued him as nothing else would have
done, but if you've had a row with him already ... he'll
never ask you to go out with him again now.'

Gemma avoided their eyes, looking into the dying
fire. Angie said her name sharply and she reluctantly
turned her head.

'All right, he did ask me to go out with him tomorrow, but I said no.'

'You did what? Gemma, how could you? You *know*
how much this experiment means to us, and it was all
going so beautifully up to now. Just what did he do
to make you so mad?'

'He—he kissed me.'

Angie stared at her disbelievingly. 'You threw everything away just because he kissed you? You must be
crazy!'

Angrily Gemma retorted, 'You weren't there, you don't know him. He's—he's so damn sure of himself. So certain that you'll find him irresistible and go to bed with him at the drop of a hat.'

'Did he ask you to sleep with him?' Lisa interrupted.

'Well, no. But he's the type that if you give him an inch he'll go the whole way,' Gemma said heatedly.

There was a tense silence until Angie asked, 'Is the option to go out with him still open?'

Gemma looked at her mutinously, then sighed. 'Yes, I suppose so.'

'Then you're going. And don't try to give me any arguments about him getting fresh again. After all, as far as he's concerned you're just an ordinary pick-up. And he's a man, isn't he? He was bound to make a pass at you. You rejected it and he wants to see you again— that must mean something. And if he makes another pass, just keep on saying no.'

'He's probably amazed that anyone could resist him,' Joy put in. 'I know I couldn't,' she added soulfully.

Lisa said slowly, 'But you aren't playing a game— that's the way you are. And sooner or later he'll realise that. And when he does, when he sees that he isn't going to get anywhere, he'll either drop you—or he'll get serious.'

Gemma gazed at them. 'You make it all sound so simple.'

'It *is* simple. When are you supposed to meet him tomorrow?'

'At ten. He said he'd take me skiing, down into Italy.'

'In that case you'd better go and get your beauty sleep.' Angie's voice was brisk now that she'd won. 'And don't worry, Gemma, we won't let the wolf devour you.'

Any secret hopes Gemma might have had for a raging blizzard were doomed to disappointment when she looked out of the window the next morning and saw that the sun was shining brightly and already there were people about in the streets. The girls chivvied her along, making her hurry over breakfast and helping her to don her disguise. They wanted her to wear Lisa's ski-suit, but she insisted on wearing her own because it fitted her better.

'You must wear your snow-goggles, Gemma, they'll help to keep the wig in place when you're skiing. Only be careful they don't dislodge it when you take them off,' Angie warned.

'All right, all right! Don't fuss.'

Already she was beginning to feel tense and edgy and by the time they got down to the village square she was ready to scream. They left her at the corner and let her make her own way into the square, but hanging around so that they could watch her. Probably to make sure I don't try to bolt, Gemma thought wryly. There was no sign of Paul and she sat on a low stone wall to wait, her skis propped up beside her. The hope that he had taken her at her word and wouldn't turn up filled her with optimism, but even as the clock in the tower of the nearby church began to strike ten, she saw a sleigh drawn by a pair of frisky, high-stepping grey horses turn into the square.

Paul sprang lightly from the sleigh and came quickly across to her. '*Bonjour*. How are you this morning?'

Gemma looked at him searchingly, ready even at this late hour to back out if he showed the slightest sign of triumph at her capitulation. But he was wearing dark glasses that effectively hid his expression and the mockery in his voice was no more than was always there. So she let him take her gear and help her into the sleigh. The driver waited impassively and Gemma gave him a quick glance, wondering if he connected her with Angie and Lisa. He had done quite well out of

their bribes up to now, although she didn't give much
for his chances of further employment if Paul ever
found out about it.

They drove out of the square, right past where the
girls were pretending to look in a shop window. Gemma
shot them a malevolent glance but had to turn back to
Paul as he started to talk to her. She had told the others
that he could be charming and now he put himself out
to display it, telling her that her luck the previous evening and her grand gesture with her winnings were now
the talk of the whole hotel.

'The receptionist wanted to get in touch with the
directors of the charity so that they could thank you
personally, but I told him that you would prefer to re-
main anonymous. Isn't that so?'

'Oh, yes,' Gemma said with heartfelt relief at having
avoided the embarrassment of such a meeting.

'Tell me,' he asked curiously, 'did you regret what
you'd done, later?'

Gemma smiled slightly, remembering the girls' reactions. 'Not really. It never seemed as if it was truly
mine, anyway. Where do we get the cable-car for the
Theodulpass?' she asked to change the subject. 'I
thought it was the other side of the village?'

'It is, but as we're rather late starting out and there
would probably be queues for the cars, I thought we
would take a quicker way up.'

He gestured ahead and Gemma saw that they were
approaching a large building with 'Heliport' written on
the front of it, and even as she watched a small helicopter, looking for all the world like a brightly hued
dragonfly, rose noisily into the air from the large
cleared area behind the building.

'You mean we're going up in a helicopter?' she
asked excitedly.

Paul looked at her in some amusement. 'Haven't you ever been up in one before?'

She shook her head, her eyes alight with pleased anticipation, her earlier tension at being with him forgotten.

He helped her out, telling the driver that he wouldn't need him again until the evening. The driver raised his whip in acknowledgement and trotted away while Paul carried their gear across to where another helicopter was waiting on the tarmac, its engine already running.

'Keep your head down,' Paul warned her as they approached it, almost shouting over the noise. He stowed their gear in a special compartment at the back and then climbed in to sit close beside her in the rather cramped double seat behind the pilot. As soon as he had strapped them both in, he tapped the pilot on the shoulder and above them the rotor blades began to bite into the air as the rev counter built up.

Gemma had been prepared for a sickening lurch when the machine took off, but it rose into the air so smoothly that she didn't know it had left the ground until she saw the heliport building start to slide past the window. She gripped the edges of the seat nervously, not yet at ease in this new element, but then she felt Paul's hand close over hers reassuringly. Quickly she turned to him, giving him a small, grateful smile and letting her hand slide into his, gripping it tightly. The helicopter gave a lurch as it turned away from the village towards the mountains and that made her stomach rise rather suddenly, but as figures and familiar places on the ground came into view she gradually lost her fears and exclaimed with pleasure.

'Oh, look! There are the cable-cars going up to Furri. How strange they look spread out like that. Rather like a jet necklace.' She prattled on until she realised that this was all old hat to Paul, that he was probably as used to riding in a helicopter as a car, and must be finding her incredibly naïve. Only then did she realise that he was still holding her hand and she immediately tried to pull free. For a moment he wouldn't let go and she was impelled to look at him. He had taken off his sunglasses and his dark eyes regarded her with an expression she couldn't quite define. He raised her hand to his lips and held it there for a moment, then let her go to point at something out of the window. They continued to fly higher into the Alps, above the slopes of the Matterhorn, and soon they had left the tree line behind and were approaching the glacier, which was already dotted with skiers.

Gemma caught her breath in wonder as she gazed at the scene. It was a fantastic experience, really out of this world. The views of the mountains were magnificent, giving an awe-inspiring feeling that a climber must have when he finally reaches the topmost peak and looks around him. It seemed hardly any time before the machine began to hover over the marked-out helipad near the alpine restaurant at Trockener Steg, which was the highest the helicopter could go because of the fear of avalanches. It took a few moments to acclimatise to the very sudden change from the warm noisy aircraft to the bright light and the cold and intense silence of the mountain, then they put on their skis and hooked themselves on to the drag-lift to take them yet higher to the very top of the pass.

'Have you ever skied on powder snow?' Paul asked her as they moved away from the top of the lift. He was referring to the natural open ground that only really good skiers attempted, away from the marked and billiard-table smooth pistes that most people used.

'Only a couple of times,' she told him, 'and not for very long distances.'

'You said you were quite a good skier—do you want to try it?'

There was a distinct note of challenge in his voice, and Gemma had never refused a reasonable challenge in her life. Her chin came up. 'Yes,' she said decisively.

Paul grinned. 'Good girl! The secret is to be really relaxed, forget all the business of adjusting your weight and just let your skis ride the snow. If you feel it's too much for you, just stop and we'll go on to the pistes. But whatever you do, don't panic. *Comprends?*'

Gemma nodded and concentrated on putting on her goggles, being careful not to dislodge her wig. He waited for her, a rather sinister figure against the pure whiteness of the snow in his black suit.

'Don't worry, I'll be right beside you.'

Taking a deep breath, Gemma set her skis towards Italy and twelve thousand feet of mountain and dug her sticks into the snow to send her speeding down.

At first she was rather nervous, not completely confident of her ability to cope, but gradually, as she became more used to the element, her confidence returned and she began to enjoy herself. She soon realised that by the merest hint of stepping from one ski to the other she could perform the most beautiful slaloms down the slope. Risking a quick look at Paul, she saw that he was keeping in position just a few yards to her left, deliberately holding back so that he could stay alongside her. They had left the marked-off piste far behind them now and it was so quiet that only the crisp sound of their skis cutting through the snow and her own breathing broke the intense stillness. Gradually Gemma began to experiment a little more, taking wide turns and looking back to see the lovely patterns she had made in the virgin snow. A feeling of exhilaration filled her, as intoxicating as champagne. At times the mountain became precipitous and she felt

as if she were hanging in mid-air, only the speed of her
momentum stopping her from falling over and over
into the valley below.

They came to a place where the snow was tough and
packed, the ground uneven. Paul swooped in front of
her then, his strong leg muscles helping him to wedel
from side to side, breaking the tough crust of the snow
so that Gemma would have an easier path. They seemed
to go on for hours, through an incredible landscape of
great ice-falls, frozen streams and endless powder snow
slopes. Gemma's legs began to tire a little, but the head-
iness of the new experience kept her going fast down
the slope. A stretch of smooth, soft snow opened before
them and she began to experiment in turns and swings,
finding it quite different here from the hard, icy sur-
faces of the pistes. This, she realised, was what true
skiing was all about; the ordinary ski-runs would never
have the same enjoyment for her again after this. She
swooped into a kangaroo turn, revelling in the stimu-
lating feeling of power it gave her, then she tried a
jet turn. Planting her stick in the snow, her body ahead
of her skis, she shot her feet forward, swinging them
round with a double knee movement and using all the
strength in her leg muscles to bring her round. The
skis sang in the still air and she laughed aloud with
sheer enjoyment.

Paul's laugh rang out alongside her and he went
down an overhanging slope to jump down several yards
and land safely. Recklessly Gemma followed him, although she could easily have gone round. She jumped
cleanly, bending her knees to take the impact on landing. The ground rose up to meet her and she hit it with
a heavy thwack. For a triumphant moment she thought
she'd done it perfectly, but then her tired calf muscles
refused to hold her and she stumbled, falling on to her
back and then beginning to roll down the sheer slope.

The safety bindings on her skis snapped open immediately and were left behind in the snow, but she managed to retain hold of her sticks, desperately trying to use them as a brake, but they were virtually useless in the soft snow.

Dimly she heard a shout behind her, but her whole being was taken up in the attempt to dig her boots into the snow, to claw her hands into it, anything to stop her from sliding any further, but her strength was spent and her struggles became more feeble.

Suddenly her feet fetched up against something solid and she rolled into a huddled ball beneath it. Dazedly Gemma opened her eyes and looked up. At first she could see nothing, and realised that her goggles were covered in snow. Raising a trembling hand, she wiped them and saw that Paul was standing there, his sticks jammed into the snow behind him, taking her weight. He had placed himself in front of her to stop her falling any further.

His voice sounded tense, unnatural, as he said, 'Are you hurt, Gemma?'

'No, I'm all right.' Slowly she felt herself, aware of aches in every part of her but no sharp pains.

'Can you get up?' His tone was still sharp.

'Yes.' She began to get to her feet, wondering why he made no attempt to help her and was still leaning his weight on his sticks.

When she was standing he seemed to relax a fraction. 'Now we are going to go slowly back up the slope. You will be just one step ahead of me and you will use your ski sticks to keep your balance, *tu comprends*?'

'Of course, but I don't see why we can't just....' Her glance went past him and she stopped dead. About five feet behind them the ground came to a sudden stop, there was just—nothing! Her fall had taken her straight to the edge of a precipice and only Paul de-

liberately using his own body as a barrier had stopped
her from going over. For a moment she swayed, feeling
sick and faint with shock.

Paul's voice, hard and urgent, brought her sharply
back to reality. 'Gemma, you mustn't faint, do you hear
me? Answer me!' he commanded roughly.

She looked up at him, her eyes large and frightened,
knowing that they were only a clumsy movement
away from death. She managed a small, tight smile.
'I—I'm all right.' Taking a firm grip on her sticks she
started to move sideways back up the slope, following
the trail of disturbed snow that showed the path of her
fall. It seemed an incredibly long way. Paul was just a
foot behind her every step of the way, ready to again
use himself as a brake if she should slip.

'That's my good girl. Not much further now,' he encouraged her, but it seemed an age before they came to
a safe, flat piece of ground and by then she was trembling with fatigue and shock. 'It's all right, we're quite
safe now,' he assured her. 'You'd better sit down and
rest.'

Gratefully Gemma sank to the ground, oblivious of
the snow that she knew would soon soak through her
padded trousers, while lifting trembling hands to take
off her ski goggles, dropping them into the snow. Paul
went away to find her skis and bring them back to her.
Kicking off his own skis, he dropped down on his knees
beside her.

'You're shaking. Here.' Pulling off his gloves, he began to massage her hands vigorously, talking to her,
trying to make her answer him, to pull her out of the
shock. 'I should have known that anyone as accident-
prone as you would have found the only precipice on
the whole mountain when she decided to take a fall.
Remind me never to take you ice-skating—the ice
would probably melt beneath your feet and I'd have to

fish you out of the water,' he said banteringly. 'How does that feel? Are you warmer now?'

'Yes.' He was rubbing her right hand and Gemma raised her left and put it over his. He stopped and looked up at her quickly. 'You—you saved my life. If you hadn't put yourself in the way—and I could so easily have taken you with me.' Her eyes looked into his, dark and troubled. 'How—how do you go about thanking someone for something like that?'

'You don't,' Paul replied brusquely, pulling her to her feet. 'You were my responsibility. I should have realised that you were out of practice and would tire easily. We'll take the rest of the way slowly, but the going is much easier from here, you shouldn't have any difficulty.' He turned away, the matter closed, but Gemma put out a hand and caught his sleeve, pulling him round to face her.

'Paul.' She gazed rather helplessly up at him, then impulsively reached up to kiss him. 'Thank you,' she murmured, and drew back.

But his arms closed round her, drawing her near. His eyes looked deep into hers for a few seconds and then lowered as he sought her mouth. His lips were insinuatingly gentle, exploring hers with little kisses as he murmured her name. She felt an impulse of sensuality that went up like a flame inside her. Obliviously she returned his embrace and as she did so, so his lips became more passionate, more intense. Ardently she responded. Paul made a small sound deep in his throat and put a hand up to her head, twining his fingers in her hair and pulling her yet closer to him.

Only after some little while did Gemma realise that the wig was starting to slide off her head, and a chill of fear and panic gripped her. It was suddenly imperative that Paul didn't find out that she'd been fooling him. She tried to pull away from him, but he immediately

drew her back again, his mouth fastening compulsively on hers as if he could never get enough, his hand
going to the zip of her suit and pulling it down.

'Paul, let me go, please!' Her voice rising sharply,
she tried to break free and then, panic-stricken as she
felt the wig slip further, 'Let me go, do you hear me?
Leave me alone!' Forcefully she pushed him away. He
stumbled a little and she had time to quickly reach up
and pull the wig back into place.

Paul rounded on her, his face angry. 'What's the
matter with you?'

Gemma said the first thing that came into her head.
'I told you—I don't like being pawed.'

'Don't lie to me, you were getting as much of a kick
out of that as I was.' He took a purposeful step towards her.

'No, that isn't true. You took advantage of me when
I was still shaken up, feeling grateful to you. Keep
away from me!'

He stopped short, shocked surprise in his eyes. 'Why,
you little ....' His jaw tightened. 'I don't know what
you're playing at, Gemma, but I warn you I don't like
little girls who play games. Did you really think I
wouldn't follow it up when you threw yourself at my
head?' he asked sneeringly.

'I'm—I'm not playing any game. It wasn't that sort
of kiss and you know it. I was grateful, that's all. Now
will you please just leave me alone?'

He continued to glare at her for a moment, then abruptly turned his back as he put on his skis. Gemma
was able to repin the wig, anchoring it in place with her
goggles, before she, too, stamped her feet into her skis.
Paul waited for her, not looking at her at all.

When she was ready he gave her the merest glance
before saying shortly, 'You'd better follow me down the
rest of the way. And don't try anything clever—that

way we might possibly get down in one piece.'

He pushed off, his face grim and remote. Gemma watched him for a moment before she fell in behind him, all the pleasure in the day completely destroyed.

CHAPTER SIX

THE foot of the mountain was reached without further mishap, and at the bottom they had to show their passports at the frontier posts as they crossed from Switzerland into Italy. In Cervinia Paul took her to a small but exclusive restaurant where they ate in an atmosphere of icy politeness. It wasn't that he ignored her—Gemma almost wished he would—it was just that he treated her as if she were someone he had been landed with and whose company he found very boring and couldn't wait to get away from. He spoke of exotic, jet-set places he'd visited and was sarcastic of her ignorance when she admitted she had never been to any of them.

At first Gemma felt hurt and humiliated by his attitude, but then anger began to creep in.

The meal finished, Paul said, 'You're obviously too tired to take the cable-car back up the Matterhorn and ski down to Zermatt, so I suggest we take a sleigh for the return journey.'

She would have liked to spend longer looking round the town, but when she nodded he immediately led the way to where a line of sleighs were waiting for hire and helped her into the first one. He sat down opposite her this time instead of beside her, and taking out a cigarette case, offered her one.

'No, thanks, I don't smoke.'

Paul took one for himself and sat back. His eyes ran over her for a moment in almost insolent appraisal, then he looked away, bored. Gemma sat silently, her hands clenched together under the rug, her anger beginning to seethe and come close to boiling point.

Okay, so maybe she had brought things to a rather abrupt conclusion back there on the mountain, but it would have ended even more abruptly if he had found out she'd been fooling him all along. But he wasn't to know that, of course; he merely thought ... what?... that she had rejected his advances again, she supposed. But he was reacting out of all proportion to the offence—like some spoiled child who'd been refused a toy. He was probably piqued because she had said no. He was so good-looking that it must be an experience he hadn't encountered very often before. But he had no cause to act this way; she had as much right to reject his advances as he had to make them.

The cigarette finished, Paul threw away the stub, and as if becoming aware of her presence, began, rather as if he was humouring a child, to point out some of the places of interest they passed.

Gemma stood it for as long as she could, but as the crossroads leading to Zermatt came into view, she said tartly, 'Don't bother!'

He raised an eyebrow. '*Comment?*'

'I said, don't bother. You don't have to put yourself out to entertain me any longer.' Turning to the driver, she told him to stop and threw aside the rugs.

'Where do you think you're going—it's almost three kilometres still to Zermatt!'

'I'd rather walk ten kilometres than spend another minute with you. You can do your sulking by yourself!'

His jaw tightened. 'I am not—sulking.'

'No? Then just what do you call it?' The sleigh had come to a stop and she jumped to the ground and went to get her ski gear. Paul immediately got out behind her and swung her round to face him, his eyes angry. The driver watched them with unconcealed interest.

'I took you out and I'll take you back, after that you

can do what you damn well like. Get back in the sleigh.'

'No! I'm not going anywhere with you. I should never have gone out with you in the first place.'

'So why did you?'

'Because I. . . .' Gemma stopped abruptly and stared at him as he glowered down at her, an exasperated expression on his face. Hastily she turned away and again reached for her skis.

'I told you, I'm taking you back,' he said furiously.

'And I told *you*, I'm not going any further with you.'

'Oh, you made *that* plain enough,' he said sarcastically, and Gemma realised that he wasn't referring to the sleigh ride at all, but the episode on the mountain.

Eyes sparkling with rage, she raised her hand to hit him, but he dodged neatly out of the way and caught her wrist. His eyes blazed at her and he said grimly, 'There's only one thing to do with you.' And the next second she was picked up bodily in his arms and he had dumped her in the sleigh, coming quickly to sit beside her and pinion her back against the seat with his arm. 'Drive on,' he told the driver, adding unpleasantly, 'And take that asinine grin off your face.'

The grin disappeared as if by magic and the horses were whipped up to a smart trot. Gemma struggled ineffectively against him, but his arm was like a steel band round her. Recognising the futility of her efforts, she gave up and glared at him angrily.

'I despise men who use brute strength to get their own way,' she told him acidly.

Caustically he replied, 'And I abhor women who thinks it's feminine to act stupidly and irrationally.'

'Then you must know some very strange women!' Gemma retorted. 'Or is it just that that synthetic charm you turn on brings out the worst in them?'

'None, I assure you, have acted as strangely as you;

and just what makes you think my manner is synthetic, as you call it?'

Gemma smiled grimly to herself; that cut had got to him, he hadn't liked it at all. 'Because you turn it on and off like a tap. A truly charming person would treat everyone the same, no matter how they acted towards him. He would be too big, too much of a man, to let others' reactions affect him.'

His arm tightened perceptibly. 'So you don't think I'm man enough for you, do you?' His eyes had narrowed and there was a dangerous look on his face.

But Gemma swept on regardless. 'No, I don't. I think you're an arrogant, conceited. . . .'

Paul's fingers closed on her throat, silencing her. His face was very close. 'You can't throw down a challenge like that and not expect me to take it up,' he said silkily. 'And I'm beginning to think it will give me a great deal of pleasure to prove to you how wrong you are.'

Gemma blinked, realising that the argument had somehow got completely out of hand. 'Why, you—you swine! That isn't what I meant and you know it. Stop this sleigh and let me out this minute. Hi, driver, stop!' But the man had suddenly become very deaf and took no notice of her. Gemma gritted her teeth in annoyance while Paul laughed openly.

'He knows he won't get a tip if he stops again.' Looking at her flushed face and angry eyes, he said abruptly, 'Why do you always fight me? Are you like this with all men?'

'That's none of your damn business!'

'Isn't it? I think it is.' She tried to turn away, but he cupped her chin and forced her to look at him. 'Why is it, Gemma? You're not afraid of me, are you?'

'No, of course not. I just don't like being—handled.'

'You liked it well enough at first. In fact, I'd say that you were enjoying it a great deal, so why pull away as you did? After all, I was hardly likely to rape you on the side of the mountain,' he added drily.

A flush of colour came to her face. 'Find another groove in the record, will you? Or do you only have a one-track mind?' she added nastily.

Paul's eyes grew angry again, but before he could speak the sleigh came to a standstill and Gemma saw with relief that they had arrived at the square. Quickly she pushed him aside and jumped out of the sleigh, reaching up for her gear. Paul made no attempt either to help or to stop her, just sitting in the sleigh, stony-faced, until she turned and began to walk hurriedly away. Behind her she heard the sleigh begin to move off in the direction of the hotel. Blindly she walked on, threading her way through the crowds. Reaching the much quieter road leading up to the chalet, she began to climb the hill. There was nothing to warn her that he had followed her, his footsteps making no sound on the snow.

Swinging her round to face him, Paul looked down at her grimly. 'You forgot your goggles.' He held them out to her.

Gemma gave a gasp of surprise when she saw him. 'Th-thank you.' She reached out and took hold of the goggles, but he didn't let go.

'You crazy little idiot! Why do you always make me so angry?' he said roughly.

There was no answering that one and Gemma stood silent.

He looked at her searchingly. 'Have you been crying?' He made it sound like an accusation.

'No! Of course not! You don't seriously think I'd cry over an arrogant swine like you, do you?' she said sharply, attack being the better form of defence.

'*Mon dieu*, give me strength!' He glared down at her. 'Are you going to come out with me tomorrow or not?'

Gemma glared back just as angrily. 'Yes, I am! Although why I should after you've....' She broke off because he had begun to laugh at her. Slowly she too began to smile, albeit reluctantly.

He took her hand and drew her to him. 'And no more arguments, *n'est-ce pas*?'

Putting her head to one side, Gemma looked up at him pertly. 'And no more cause for them?'

He appeared to deliberate the point. 'Well, perhaps just friendly arguments.' They laughed together and he put his arm round her waist. 'I'll walk you to your chalet.'

Too quickly she said, 'I can manage alone, thanks.'

Putting his hands on her shoulders, Paul looked closely into her face. 'Gemma, are you married?'

Eyes wide, she looked back at him in astonishment. 'Good heavens, no! Did you think I was?'

'Not engaged or anything?'

'No. There's no one. Why did you think there was?'

He shrugged. 'Your reluctance to let me take you home.'

'No, it's as I said—I'm staying with friends, three *girl* friends,' she emphasised. 'And they'd—well, they'd tease me about you, want to know about you.'

'And you don't want to tell them?'

'No.'

For once the cynicism was gone from his face as he said, 'All right, Gemma, have it your way. I'll meet you in the square again tomorrow, but don't bother to bring skis this time.' Then he bent and drew back her glove to kiss her wrist very lightly. His eyes met hers, and then he was gone, pausing at the corner to look back and give a casual wave.

The next week seemed to fly by all too exhilaratingly fast. She saw Paul every day, often during the daytime and again in the evening. They watched ski-jump

competitions and went tobogganing, had an unforget-
table ride on a snow-cat and visited a hang-gliding
school where Gemma watched enviously while Paul
expertly piloted his brightly-coloured glider, taking
advantage of the air currents to fly slowly down from
the mountain and land safely on his skis on the valley
floor.

As soon as he was down she ran excitedly to him.
'That looked fantastic! How did it feel? Is it very
difficult? How do you make it come down?'

Taking off his safety helmet, Paul put his arm round
her, laughing at her bubbling enthusiasm. 'Would you
like to try it? I'll teach you.'

'But it must take several lessons before you can actually fly, mustn't it?'

'Yes, so we might as well start at once.'

He proved to be a good instructor and before the end
of the afternoon Gemma had successfully taken off
and glided down a gentle ten-foot slope, miraculously
managing not to hurt herself or anyone else.

'We'll have you flying within a month,' Paul pro-
phesied.

In a month? He spoke with assurance, as if he took
it for granted that they would still be going together
that long. Gemma stayed silent; in a month's time she
would be back in Oxford, attending lectures and studying hard. It was something she didn't think about
often, deliberately pushing it to the back of her mind.
She was enjoying herself too much; enjoying the places
Paul took her to, and—she had to admit it—taking
pleasure in just being with him. She had never known
anyone like him before; he was so sure of himself, so
decisive; deferential to her preferences, but seeming to
know instinctively what would please her, so that she
never felt that she was being organised. The thought
that he probably knew what she would like because of

his past experience with other women she also resolutely pushed out of her mind.

In the evenings he took her out to dinner at restaurants where the food was always of gourmet quality, or to nightclubs where they danced into the small hours. But when they again tried the Casino, Gemma found that her luck had completely deserted her. She lost ten times in a row and refused to play any more, giving up her seat to Paul and being content to watch instead. When he won she put a congratulatory hand on his arm, his own came up to cover it and his glance met hers over his shoulder. Abruptly he stood up and pocketed his chips, taking her hand to lead her to the dance floor.

They seemed to talk a lot, and yet, when Gemma looked back on their conversations, she realised that she had learned very little about Paul. He would speak knowledgeably on books, music, art, but was strangely reticent about his past and his business interests. She gathered that he had been born in Provence, but that his parents had separated when he was still very young, and his father had so arranged his business empire that it virtually ran itself. A director of the holding company came every few weeks with progress reports and papers for him to sign and that was all Paul had to do to maintain his luxurious life-style.

Gemma was equally reticent; talking freely and naturally of her life back home in Norfolk with her family, but clamming up at once if the more recent past was mentioned. Paul might wonder about her silence and speculate on it, but he didn't probe, respecting her right to privacy as she respected his. Their range of topics was varied, and although Gemma tried not to, it was inevitable that her knowledge and learning sometimes came out, particularly when they talked about books. His eyes would narrow then and he would look at her quickly, thoughtfully, especially when he found out that she could speak French as fluently as he could speak English.

And he kept his word about not making a pass at her again. He kissed her often when they were alone, but had always kept himself under control and stopped when she had drawn away, flushed and breathless from his embrace. His eyes would look at her in wry mockery, but he was content for the moment to wait.

Her disguise had almost become a part of her now. It was almost as if whenever she put it on, she walked on to a vast stage and took part in a rather wonderful play, only returning to normal when she removed it, or when Angie brought her rudely back to earth by demanding details of her meetings with Paul for her notes. Rather reluctantly Gemma gave the bare essentials, but luckily Angie didn't want to know too much; just where they'd been and whether Paul had said anythink to indicate his feelings about her.

Angie and Lisa had met two British skiers who were in Zermatt to train in the hope of getting in the next Olympic team, while Joy's friendship with her Italian instructor was really hotting up. So much of the time they all went their separate ways, only Angie continuing to do any actual work on the experiment. But after about a week of this she insisted they all get back to the chalet early one afternoon so that they could have a conference.

'Look, this just isn't good enough,' she pointed out. 'You've all gone so man crazy that you're in danger of forgetting why we came here in the first place.'

Indignantly Joy said, 'You've been going out with a man too.'

'Only because I'd have been left by myself all day if I hadn't,' Angie retorted loftily, adding hastily as she saw the sparks in Joy's eyes, 'But that's neither here nor there. The point is that we've only got just over two weeks of our holiday left, and Paul Verignac doesn't seem to be getting anywhere near the point of proposing to Gemma.'

'I've been going out with him for less than two weeks,' Gemma protested. 'And he's a hardened bachelor, remember? You can hardly expect him to change his outlook so quickly.' She wished heartily that Angie would leave them alone, but she knew that she had no right to say so; if it hadn't been for them she would never have met Paul.

'I know that,' Angie was saying. 'So I thought that at this stage we needed more help from the computer. I telephoned a friend in the university computer section who collaborated with me on the earlier work I did. He fed in all the latest data and phoned me back with the results this morning.' She pushed her glasses back on to her nose and prepared to read from her notebook. 'It suggests that to make Mr X propose more quickly we use shock tactics. Possibly by making him jealous.'

At once Gemma exclaimed vehemently, 'No!'

They looked at her in some astonishment. 'Why on earth not?' Lisa asked her.

Gemma tried to marshal her reasons after her hasty decision and said gropingly, 'Because it wouldn't work. The computer's wrong this time. Paul just isn't the type of man who'd let a woman treat him that way. If I showed an interest in another man he would finish it there and then, just walk away and I'd never see him again.'

The others exchanged glances and Lisa said, 'Well, that's out, then. It would have been terribly difficult to set up anyway,' she added as a sop to Angie's disappointment. 'We'll just have to think of something else.'

'But what?'

They thought for a while until Joy said, 'Perhaps if Gemma tells him she's got to leave in two weeks, that might bring him to the point.'

'Why should it?' Angie returned. 'He's rich enough to follow her back to England to get to know her better, and we don't want that. No, we must find a way of making him propose while we're still in Switzerland.'

'How about if we put Gemma in mortal danger—from an avalanche or something—and let him rescue her?' Joy suggested, letting her imagination run away with her.

'And just how are we supposed to arrange an avalanche? Besides, Gemma might get killed.'

'Well, you have to take some risks in the name of science.'

Gemma, who was sitting next to Joy, immediately made a grab at her, pulling her off her chair and trying to sit on her, yelling to Lisa to put a snowball down her neck, and the meeting would have degenerated into a highly enjoyable but very unladylike romp if Angie hadn't called them back to order.

'Stop it, you two! We've got to think of something.'

'I've had an idea that might work,' Lisa informed them. 'Why doesn't Gemma herself provide the shock?' They all turned to her, their attention held by a hint of excitement in her voice. 'What Paul Verignac needs is stirring up a bit, right? Up to now Gemma's been just a nice girl whom he's enjoyed taking around. But how about if we let him see that there's more to her than that, drop the aura of mystery a bit? Let him see that when she lets her hair down she can be an exciting, scintillating, sexy woman.'

'You're using all the wrong adjectives,' Gemma said drily. 'I could never be all those things if I tried.'

'Yes, you could,' Lisa answered confidently. 'I'll teach you.'

'How would you know?' Joy asked. 'You're not like that either.'

'No, but I know how to act like it. I learnt for a play I was in once.'

'And could you teach Gemma?'

'Of course. By the time I've finished with her Paul Verignac won't know what's hit him!'

She began at once while the others watched avidly. First she made Gemma walk up and down the room, but shook her head in disapproval. 'No, you must move more like this,' she demonstrated. 'The top half of your body leaning back a little, and you must move your hips more. No, not that much—that looked much too overdone. You just want enough emphasis to let him know you're a woman, Try putting one foot in *front* of the other when you walk instead of parallel. That's it! That's much better.'

After Gemma had mastered this to her satisfaction, Lisa made her pick up a glass and hold it. 'Now when he's talking to you, slowly run your finger tip round the rim of the glass a few times, then lower your fingers to caress the bowl. It's tremendously sensual to fondle something. And when you drink, do it slowly and look at him over the edge.'

'You don't seriously expect me to do all that, do you? I'll look ridiculous,' Gemma protested.

'Try it,' Lisa urged. 'It's really very effective.'

And when Gemma had practised it and watched herself in the mirror, she had to admit that Lisa was right.

'When he talks to you open your eyes wide as if you're terribly interested, and occasionally let your eyes run over him—you know, the way a man does to a girl.'

'Lisa, this is Paul Verignac I'm meeting, remember? Acting like this could be dangerous.'

'No, it won't. You'll only be hinting at the possibility

of things to come, he's not going to get any goodies until he proposes—or so he'll think. Another thing you might do is to gently stroke your bare arm, running your fingers from your elbow right up to your shoulder. And run the tip of your tongue across your lips.'

The girls looked at her in something approaching awe. 'Did you really learn all this for a play?' Joy asked, fascinated.

'Well, no, that last bit I saw in a film once, but it was so sexy that I've always remembered it. Try it, Gemma.'

Lisa made her rehearse all the afternoon and later inspected all the evening dresses they'd brought with them to find something suitable, i.e. sexy, for Gemma to wear, eventually choosing a black dress of Angie's which had a tight-fitting underdress with floating chiffon panels over the top.

'This will do, although you won't be able to wear a bra under it, and the panels will have to come off, of course,' she declared.

'Lisa, that is my newest evening dress. I've only worn it twice,' Angie wailed.

'Huh! And who was it said you should be willing to make any sacrifice in the cause of science?' Joy said gleefully.

'Don't worry, we'll sew them on again,' Lisa assured her. 'There, with my white boa round your neck, that should look okay. I'll give you a bit more make-up tonight and I think you should wear the wig long and flicking back into soft curls.'

The whole effect was stunning. Gemma gazed at herself in the long mirror, knowing that the glamorous creature who stared back at her was herself, and yet somehow not believing it. She looked at her reflection for several minutes and then took off the boa and flung it on a chair. 'No,' she said decisively. 'I'm not going to do it. We're getting along fine as we are and that will have to satisfy you. What you want me to do is too dangerous. It's asking for trouble.'

'Wait,' said Angie hastily. 'Don't make any rash decisions. You can always say no, can't you?'

Gemma rounded on her. 'Angie, this whole set-up is a come-on. If you think Paul Verignac is going to pass it up—then your computer wants re-programming!' she declared crossly.

'Wait a minute, let's think,' Lisa intervened. 'Gemma, would you be willing to try this if you were sure there wouldn't be any danger of his seducing you?'

'I don't think it's necessary at all. Why can't we just wait and see what develops?'

'Because we haven't got time. We went into all that,' Angie pointed out impatiently. 'And it was you who refused to make him jealous.'

'Would you, Gemma?' Lisa persisted, completely ignoring Angie.

Gemma looked at them mutinously. 'Oh, all right, I suppose so, but only if you can guarantee it. How do you propose to stop him?'

'He'll have to get you back to his chalet if he wants to try anything, right?'

'Yes, I should think so.'

'So all you have to do is to make sure he doesn't take you back there until about a quarter to twelve. At midnight exactly I'll phone the hotel and ask them to put me through. When he answers I'll invent an excuse so that you have to leave immediately. How does that grab you? You can hold him off for fifteen minutes, can't you?'

'I suppose so,' Gemma admitted, but looked at them unhappily.

'I've got a silver watch that will go with that outfit, then you'll know what the time is,' Lisa offered, and ran upstairs to get it. When she came back and was fastening it on, Gemma made one last try.

'I really don't want to do this. It's all wrong. Please don't....'

But Angie interrupted her brusquely. 'You promised to go along with the experiment all the way, Gemma. You can't back out now.'

'Give her a drink,' Joy suggested. 'That should make her feel better. Listen, isn't that the horse-taxi we ordered?'

They bustled around her; Joy pushing a drink into her hand while Lisa held her fur coat for her to put on. Hastily Gemma swallowed the drink and nearly choked when she realised it was neat gin. Before she knew where she was they had pushed her outside and she was in the sleigh, the neat spirit exploding like cannon balls in her head.

When she reached the hotel Paul was waiting in the entrance and swung up beside her, and Gemma felt a great wave of relief when she realised that they wouldn't be dining in the hotel restaurant. Drawing the rug over himself, Paul put an arm round her and drew her close to him, lowering his head to smell her perfume.

'Mm, you smell delicious.' His lips, feather-light, just touched her neck, the curve of her chin.

Gemma felt her heart give a silly kind of lurch and her pulse began to race. Rather breathlessly she asked, 'Where are we going?'

'I booked a table at a nightclub outside the village. You know, the one where you had an argument with my car,' he added mockingly.

And not only with his car, Gemma thought, remembering the incident only too well. It had been the start of everything really, because after that he had deliberately sought her out. As if he guessed her thoughts, Paul's arm tightened around her. She turned her head to look at him; as usual he was bareheaded, he never wore a hat even when it was snowing. The soft glow of the sleigh lanterns hardly reached to them, but she could see that he was looking at her intently. As she watched a strange light came into his eyes, but before she could attempt to fathom it he had bent to kiss her. She returned it ardently; she couldn't help herself, she never had been able to with him, and they didn't draw apart until the sleigh came to a standstill at the big car-park outside Zermatt.

His car was already warmed up and waiting for them, and it took only a short time to get to the nightclub, Gemma going straight to the cloakroom to repair her lipstick. When she came out, the boa slung negligently over her shoulders, Paul straightened, his eyes quickening with interest.

'Ma belle,' he murmured as he possessively put her hand on his arm. 'Tu es très charmante ce soir.'

Every eye seemed to be on them as they walked to their table, and Gemma flushed, acutely aware of the figure-hugging dress. When their aperitifs came, she drank hers down to still her trembling hands. For the moment she had pushed all Lisa's lessons to the back of her mind, talking to Paul quite normally, but then she saw him raise his glass as he acknowledged someone behind her. Turning, Gemma saw that it was the woman she had once seen him with, the one who had reputedly left her husband for him. The woman ran her eyes over Gemma and raised a disdainful eyebrow. Her face tight, Gemma turned back to Paul.

'An old flame?' she asked lightly.

He looked at her in some amusement. 'Do I detect a note of jealousy?'

'Certainly not!' Gemma tossed her head and lifted her chin defiantly.

Paul laughed outright. 'Don't lie to me. It's written

in every line of your lovely face. And why try to hide it? It's a natural reaction. Anyway, I rather like my women to be jealous.'

Her eyes flashed at him. 'I am *not* one of your women!'

'*Doucement!*' He put his hand on her arm and pulled her back into her chair as she half rose to leave. 'No, you're not. And neither is she an old flame,' he added. The waiters came with their first course then and he waited until she had raised her fork to her mouth before he added wickedly, 'She's more of a burnt-out volcano!'

If he hadn't said that, Gemma might not have resorted to Lisa's tricks, but she decided that Paul deserved a much-needed lesson. After they had eaten she held her brandy glass as she'd been shown, and by that time she had had enough to drink to really do it well, uncaring of the consequences. When they threaded their way to the dance floor she was in front of him and she remembered to walk as Lisa had demonstrated. At first it didn't seem to have any effect on Paul, but when they sat down again and she began to, apparently absent-mindedly, stroke her arm, her eyes wide, her mouth slightly open to display the tip of her tongue, he seemed to forget what he was saying and stopped for long seconds to gaze at her, eyes narrowed. He recovered himself, but afterwards watched her more closely, a speculative expression in his eyes.

When they went to the dance floor, Paul held her very close to him, his hands low on her waist. For a moment she stiffened, then relaxed, her arms going up around him, her fingers playing idly with the silky hair that curled at the base of his neck. She was playing with fire, she knew, as she felt his arms tighten about her, and she would never have dared to do it if she hadn't known that Lisa would come to her rescue. And because she knew it was safe, she could enjoy the power she had to arouse him. Any inhibitions she might have felt had disappeared with the drinks she had consumed, and now she experienced a strange kind of fascination to test her powers, to see how far she could go and how Paul would react. So she moved yet closer to him, her head on his shoulder.

'*Chérie*, let's leave, shall we?' His voice sounded unsteady.

'Already?' Gemma glanced at Lisa's watch and was surprised to see that it was ten-thirty; she had thought it was earlier than that. She pretended to pout. 'But it's early yet and I'm enjoying myself. There's plenty of time, isn't there? We've got all night.'

His hand came up to grip her wrist. 'Gemma....'

But she smiled and put her fingers against his lips, stopping him. 'Later.'

His eyes met hers and he gave a slow, knowing smile.

After they had had another drink they danced again, but halfway through Paul suddenly moved away from her. 'We're leaving now,' he said abruptly and led her firmly from the floor.

In the cloakroom Gemma again checked her watch; just after eleven. She calculated that it would take over half an hour to get back to Zermatt so they should arrive at about the right time. In the car, of course, Paul had to give all his attention to his driving, but once in the sleigh it was a different matter. He spoke to the driver in German, telling him to hurry, not realising that Gemma understood, and once beside her he lost no time in taking her in his arms and kissing her hungrily, his lips bruising in their intensity.

'Oh, Gemma, you're so wonderful tonight. Devastating.' His hand sought the opening of her coat, but she held him off.

'No, not yet. Not here.'

Unwillingly he obeyed, and kissed her so passionately that the world was whirling round her and she
didn't even realise they had arrived when the sleigh
pulled up at the chalet.

That his chalet was luxurious was an understate-
ment; it was split level with a dining area in the upper
part set in front of a huge picture window that in the
daytime must give a superb view of the Alps, and on the
lower level there were big, comfortable sofas set round
a great fireplace piled with logs that were already lit
and throwing out a warm, crackling glow. Paul hadn't
turned on the lights and Gemma only dimly noticed
a carved staircase leading up to a galleried landing. But
she hardly had time to look round before Paul had
come up behind her to help her with her coat. He
dropped it on a chair and then pulled her hard back
against him, his hands gripping her shoulders.

'Gemma, do you know what you're doing?' His voice
sounded harsh in her ears.

For answer she turned slowly round to face him. For
a long moment she gazed at him and then reached up
to bring his head down and kiss him lingeringly. Soon
he picked her up and carried her to the sofa in front of
the fire, and as he did so she looked again at the time.
Seven minutes to midnight. For seven minutes she was
going to forget everything else and let herself find out
what it was like to be loved by a man.

Sitting on the sofa, he laid her across him, kissing
her eyes, her neck, murmuring endearments in French,
his English forgotten, while his hands began to explore
her body. He had already taken off his jacket and now
Gemma reached up to undo his bow tie, dropping it
on the floor, then very deliberately she undid the but-
tons of his shirt, letting her hands slide inside to touch
his smooth, bare skin. His breathing quickened and
she could feel his heart hammering beneath her hand.

He gave a kind of groan deep in his throat and his mouth fastened compulsively on hers.

Somehow she found that they had rolled on to the big goatskin rug in front of the hearth. The fire flickered and glowed, sending weird shadows round the room. Paul's hand went to the zip at the back of her dress, slowly pulling it down. Gemma let him because it was almost midnight. Any second now the phone would ring. His fingers traced the outline of her spine, gently exploring. Gemma moaned and moved sensuously against him.

'Gemma, my darling.' His voice was hoarse and ragged. 'I want to be closer to you. I want to love you.' He began to slip the dress down over her breasts, his lips following it. Gemma forgot the phone, forgot everything in the ecstasy of the sensations he aroused in her.

It was a pin from her wig digging into her head that brought her back to her senses. She became suddenly aware of what was happening and knew with sickening clarity that if she didn't stop it now, it would be too late. 'No! No, please!' Somehow she found the strength to throw Paul off and scramble to her feet, her hands fumbling to pull up her dress and do up the zip.

He came to his feet in one quick movement and stared at her from the other side of the fireplace. 'What the hell are you playing at?' His voice was rough, and out of control.

'I—I have to leave.' Desperately she looked round for her shoes, but before she could move to pick them up, he was beside her, his fingers biting cruelly into her arms.

'*What* did you say?'

'I have to leave. Oh, Paul, please try to understand.'

'What the hell is it with you?' His eyes blazed down at her and she shrank away from him. 'First you behave like a frigid little schoolgirl, the next like a sex-crazy

siren. Do you get some sort of perverted pleasure out
of blowing first hot and then cold, is that it?'

'No. I—I just can't. I'm sorry.'

'You're *sorry*!' He let her go suddenly, almost pushing her away from him so that she stumbled. 'Do you
know what you're doing to me?'

Her breath was coming in frightened little sobs and
she couldn't answer him. He took a few paces round the
room like an angry caged animal while he sought to
control himself. Gemma found her shoes and put them
on, took two steps towards the door to pick up her
coat.

'Oh, no, you don't. You're not going anywhere until
we have this thing out.' Paul moved with suppressed
violence, catching her arm and dragging her back in
front of the fire where he could see her, jerking her
round to face him.

'Do you want me to force you, is that it? Are you the
kind that needs to be raped every time before you get
any satisfaction out of it? Because it appeases your feelings of guilt?' he asked savagely. 'Well, I'm sorry to dis-
appoint you, but I've never yet taken a woman against
her will and I don't intend to start with you!'

Gemma gazed at him in horror. 'No! No, that's not
true. That's a revolting thing to say!' She tried to pull
away from him, but he only tightened his hold.

'Then why, Gemma? Why?'

She stared up at him, her eyes wide and frightened,
knowing that she was by no means out of danger yet.
'Because—because I've never . . . never. . . .' She stopped,
unable to go on, head bent, her cheeks flaming.

'Because you've never been with a man before, is
that what you're trying to say?' He put his hand under
her chin, forcing her to look at him.

Slowly, reluctantly, she nodded.

His eyes grew hard, murderous. 'And so you decided

that you'd use me to make you a woman, did you? And that's what all that sex play tonight was all about—to turn me on, wasn't it? Wasn't it?' he repeated savagely, twisting her wrist when she didn't answer.

'No! I don't know. Oh, Paul, please let me go!'

But he pulled her roughly against him. His shirt was still open and she could feel his skin against her bare arms. Her eyes swimming with tears, she looked pleadingly up at him.

'*Mon dieu*, haven't you learned yet not to make promises that you can't follow through? What made you do it, Gemma? Were you curious to find out what sex was really like—or did you just feel left out because your girl-friends were sleeping around and you weren't?' he sneered. 'Well, all right, throw your virginity away if you want to, but I resent being cold-bloodedly chosen as your guinea-pig! Go home and grow up, Gemma. And next time you make it plain to a man that you're for sale, just remember that he might not let you go when you realise that you're too much of a coward to go through with it.'

He glared down at her, his eyes contemptuous, and then he stepped back abruptly. 'Now get out of here. Get out before I forget that you're just an immature little girl who can't make up her mind whether or not she wants to be a woman!'

Her hand to her mouth, Gemma stared at him for a long moment, then she turned with a sob to pick up her coat. As she ran out of the door she heard the phone begin to ring.

CHAPTER SEVEN

The Chalet Domino was in darkness, the others not having returned from their dates, and as soon as Gemma had let herself in, she ran to her room and threw herself on the bed, huddled into a small, trembling ball. Tears of shame and humiliation ran down her cheeks as she remembered his angry accusations and the way he had handled her. Her cheeks grew hot as she relived the sensations he had aroused in her, sensations that she hadn't known she was capable of feeling until tonight, and in which it would have been so easy to be lost, to have just let him do what he wanted. And what she wanted too, she realised ashamedly. Even as she thought of it, her body longed for the touch of his hands, his lips.

Restlessly she turned, digging her fingers into the bedspread. If she hadn't stopped him, if she'd let him go on. . . . But luckily she had come to her senses in time. And lucky, too, that Paul had let her go so easily. But no, that wasn't fair. It wasn't luck; somehow she had known instinctively that he would respect her wishes even at that stage of the game, that he wouldn't force himself on her. But why she had been so sure when it was well known that Paul took any woman he wanted, she couldn't begin to fathom. Downstairs the front door banged and she heard footsteps running up the stairs before there was a peremptory knock and Lisa came in.

'Gemma, are you all right? What happened? He didn't. . . . Oh, God, he didn't. . .?'

Gemma rolled to the edge of the bed and sat up, her

face averted. 'No, I'm all right. Why didn't you phone?' she asked dully.

'But I *did*. He said you'd already left. He sounded terribly angry, so I came back here straightaway. But surely you didn't get that far in a quarter of an hour?'

'Of course not, we were there much longer. Look, it's after one,' Gemma pointed out, lifting her watch for Lisa to see.

'But it's only....' Lisa broke off abruptly, her face showing growing distress. 'Oh, Gemma, I'm so terribly sorry! It's all my fault. I haven't worn that watch since we've been here and I forgot to alter it to Swiss time.'

For a moment Gemma stared at her, then she slowly began to laugh, little hiccuping giggles that suddenly gave way to sobs. Immediately Lisa put her arms round her.

'That swine! What did he do to you?'

Gemma shook her head, mopping at her tears with a tissue and trying hard to control herself. 'Nothing. He let me go when I ... when I said no. But he was so angry, Lisa, although I asked for every word of it, and he made me feel so—so childish! But at least it's over. He won't want to come within a mile of me after this. I know you'll all be disappointed that the experiment failed, but, let's face it, it was doomed from the start. No man in Paul Verignac's position would ever contemplate marrying what to him must be a complete nobody; there are far too many more eligible girls around for that. And at least I won't have to wear these any more.' She took out the lenses and replaced them carefully in their box, then took the pins out of the wig and held it in her hands for a minute before resolutely shutting it away in a drawer.

'And now we'll be able to enjoy the next two weeks without any worries and I can be myself again,' she said over-brightly. 'I've worn that darn wig so much that I was beginning to forget who I really was.' Managing a weak smile, she added, 'Lisa, I'm awfully tired. Would you mind if I went to bed now?'

'Of course.' Lisa rose at once. 'And don't worry about telling Joy and Angie, I'll explain what happened. I know it isn't easy, but try to forget what happened, Gemma. I feel so guilty about it.'

'Don't be. It was bound to happen sooner or later. We were just idiots to think that we could get away with it, that's all. Goodnight, Lisa.'

But although she had spoken the truth when she said she was tired, Gemma still lay awake long after she had heard Joy and Angie come in and the soft murmur of their voices as they talked to Lisa, followed by the slight noises they made as they crept up to bed, trying hard not to disturb her. And the uselessness of their efforts showed on her face when she came down to breakfast the next morning; in the dark shadows under her eyes and the pinched look round her mouth. After one swift glance at her the girls were careful to avoid any reference to the experiment and instead talked of other things.

'What shall we do today?' Angie asked. 'I thought perhaps we could go to the mountaineering museum this morning—we haven't seen that yet—and possibly hire a couple of toboggans this afternoon. What do you think?'

Lisa and Joy immediately made enthusiastic noises, and Gemma realised that they were going to try and cheer her up whether she wanted it or not. She made a weak effort to be left alone. 'Look, I'm sure you all have dates for today. There's no need to break them on my account; I shall be quite happy to just stay here by myself. I've got lots of washing and that to catch up on, and I really ought to write a letter home.'

'We're not going to go out and leave you moping here

alone,' Joy said forcibly. 'We all stick together. If you don't want to go out, then we'll *all* stay here.'

So after that she had no choice but to go with them, and if they did break any dates they were tactful enough not to let her overhear them. They kept her busy all that day, going from the museum to a popular restaurant for lunch and then on to hire a couple of toboggans which they found great fun, even though they all collected a few bruises in the course of the afternoon. And in the evening they went to a disco where the men they had been dating turned up, one of them 'just happening' to have a friend in tow who was without a date.

Gemma saw through their stratagem at once, but went along with it. It had been done with the best of intentions, she knew; to take her mind off Paul and to bring her back into the swing of things, but for one of the few times in her life she wished that they would leave her alone; she needed a little time to herself to sort out the mixed-up emotions and new aspects of herself that Paul had laid bare.

But the girls were determined not to leave her by herself and the next morning they decided that they would spend the day on the mountains, having some advanced skiing lessons. As they made their way through the village to the cable-car lift, Joy, who was walking in front, suddenly gave an exclamation and stopped dead so that Lisa, who was immediately behind, cannoned into her.

'Hey, what is it? You haven't forgotten your lift pass again, have you?'

'No,' Joy answered hurriedly. 'I mean yes, I think I have. We'd better go back for it.' She started to turn away, pulling at Gemma to come with her while trying to hide the frantic messages she was signalling with her eyes to Angie and Lisa.

'What on earth...? Oh, yes, I think you're right.'

Angie, too, tried to pull Gemma away.

But it was too late; Gemma had already looked over
Joy's shoulder and seen Paul further down the street.
He wasn't wearing a ski-suit, just dark trousers and a
bulky sweater, and he seemed to be in a hurry, walking
purposefully along towards his hotel, but when he came
to a side road, he paused and looked up it searchingly
before going on. The girls immediately crowded round
Gemma, protecting her from his sight as he passed. She
felt her heart jerk crazily and felt a pulse in her temple
begin to throb, a sure sign that she was nervous, and
it was quite a long time later before she even began to
relax, although afterwards she chided herself for being
so silly; he couldn't possibly have recognised her without her disguise.

During the next three days they saw him twice more:
once when they were about to get off a cable-car at
Schwarzsee they caught sight of him standing against
the wall of the cable-station, apparently waiting for
someone, because he was watching everyone who got
on or off, so they tacitly stayed on the cable-car and went
up to the next stop. The second time Gemma found
even more unnerving. They were at the disco Le Village one night with their various escorts, sitting round a
table and trying to make conversation over the noise of
the music. Gemma leaned forward to listen to something Lisa was saying and out of the corner of her eye
saw the door open and Paul come in. He was alone,
dressed casually but well in a tan suede suit. He looked
round the crowded room and then came further in to
order a drink, leaning against a pillar and letting his
eyes run over the dancers and then the tables as he
drank it. Gemma lowered her head, her fingers gripping her glass tightly as his eyes travelled towards them.
Her escort chose that moment to put his arm round her,
which helped to obscure her from Paul's view, and

when she finally found the courage to look over his
shoulder she saw that Paul had gone.

From then on she was jumpy and on edge for the rest
of the evening, drinking more than she should and yet
staying completely sober, and snapping loudly at her
date when his hands began to wander when he kissed
her goodnight, instead of warding him off in a civilised
and friendly manner. The others, she knew, looked at
her in surprise, and she was sure that they discussed her
when she wasn't with them. Gemma knew herself that
she was behaving irrationally; she ought to be glad
that the charade was over and she could be herself
again, but she began to heartily wish that the holiday
would soon end and she could go home.

The next day it snowed all day long, but the following morning they woke to brilliant sunshine again and
the girls immediately decided they must take advantage
of the weather to go skiing on the pistes while the snow
was still soft. Gemma didn't care much either way, but
the last thing she wanted to do was to spoil the others'
enjoyment, so she put on as good a face as she could
and hurried to get into her ski-suit. It was colder this
morning, so she tucked her hair into a hat that she
pulled down over her ears.

The dazzle of the sun against the new snow was very
strong and they all put on their dark glasses as they
went up in the chair-lift to Sunnegga. There was a
queue waiting for the drag-lift to take them higher and
they stood patiently in line, their backs turned to the
nearby restaurant where people were already sitting out
in the sun drinking coffee. Gemma was chatting in-
consequentially to Lisa when she thought she heard
someone call her name. But they were near a nursery
slope where people were calling out to one another all
the time and she realised she must have been mistaken.
But then it came again, nearer now and more urgent.

Gemma started to turn towards the restaurant, but before she could do so someone caught hold of her arm and spun her round.

'Gemma!'

She found herself staring into Paul's face, so shocked by his sudden appearance that she was unable to even think straight, let alone answer him. He tried to draw her away from the others but she held back, and put up a trembling hand to remove her sunglasses. He had been about to say something else, but he stopped abruptly and then moved to roughly yank the hat from her head so that her hair tumbled about her shoulders, the sun catching it and emphasising its rich chestnut glow.

Immediately a shutter came down over his face and it became a tight, unreadable mask, his tone one of polite apology. 'I beg your pardon, mademoiselle. I mistook you for a friend of mine who has a ski-suit exactly like yours.'

He walked quickly away, not looking back, and Gemma stood staring after him until Lisa pulled her back into the queue. She was strangely quiet for the rest of the day, a member of the foursome and yet not completely with them, part of her so engrossed in her own thoughts that they had to continually put themselves out to gain her attention. The others, too, were unusually quiet, looking first at Gemma and then at each other. They didn't say anything, but they certainly thought a lot!

Gemma refused to go out with them that evening, insisting that she had lots of things she wanted to catch up with, and the others didn't press her, accepting the half-truth, but knowing full well that she was afraid of running into Paul again. That the girls had discussed her was inevitable, but she didn't realise just how thoroughly and to what effect until the next day.

She had assumed that they would be going skiing again, but Joy suggested they all go down to the lake.

'If you remember, Gemma, you promised to give me a skating lesson some time.'

'I don't mind,' Gemma shrugged. 'How about you two?'

Lisa and Angie were agreeable, so they all went to change into ordinary slacks and anoraks.

'Has anyone seen my hat and sunglasses?' Gemma asked as she ran down the stairs. 'I can't find them anywhere.'

All three helped her search but couldn't find any trace of them.

'Perhaps you left them in the sleigh yesterday?' Angie suggested. 'You'll have to go without.'

'But it's terribly cold down on the lake, my ears will freeze if I don't cover them, and the glare from the ice hurts your eyes.'

'Well, you never wore them when you had your wig and lenses,' Lisa pointed out. 'Why not wear those?'

'Oh, darn, I suppose I shall have to. But help me have one more search first.'

Dutifully they helped her to look, but gave up after ten minutes and stood impatiently in the hallway while she was still searching.

At last Lisa said, 'It's no good, Gemma, you must have lost them. And we don't have any spares to lend you. You'll just have to wear the wig and contact lenses.'

'But what if Paul sees me?'

'Oh, he won't, he's always up in the mountains. Do hurry up, Gemma, if we don't get there early we'll have to queue,' Angie said impatiently.

Reluctantly she obeyed them. She had become so used to putting on the wig that it only took her a couple of minutes and it was as comfortable as any hat, and the lenses she had become expert with too.

When they reached the lake they were pleased to find

that it wasn't too crowded, only a few dozen people
gliding, with varying degrees of skill, over the smooth,
shining surface of the frozen water. In one corner an
instructor was trying to teach a class of children and
had to repeat everything in four languages before they
all understood, by which time the first lot had forgotten
it. And over on the far side several people were playing
a game of curling, the heavy stones gliding straight and
smooth over the swept ice. There was the inevitable
line of people waiting to be fitted with skates; and
they all agreed that the only drawback to a skiing holiday in a popular resort was that you always spent ages
waiting in queues. Slowly they moved forward, looking
impatiently to see how many people there were in front
of them.

'Oh, I've just remembered,' Angie exclaimed, 'I
meant to call in at the post office on the way to get some
stamps. I might as well go now rather than wait here. It
shouldn't take all that long.'

Lisa said, 'I might as well come with you, I hate
standing in line. If you get your skates before we get
back you can start giving Joy her lesson, Gemma.'

They went off together and Gemma and Joy gradually moved to the head of the line and had been served
with their skates before the others returned.

'They'll just have to go to the end of the queue
again,' said Joy as she pulled on her boots. 'Now promise you won't let go until I've got the feel of it
again.'

'I won't,' Gemma assured her as she took her arm and
helped her on to the ice. 'Now remember, lean slightly
forward and put your weight first on one leg and then
on the other.'

They went slowly round with Joy rapidly gaining
confidence as Gemma encouraged her, and soon she
was able to go along by herself with Gemma hovering
nearby.

'Concentrate on what you're doing,' Gemma rebuked her as she stumbled. 'You keep looking back towards the village.'

'I was just wondering if the others were coming. Show me how to turn.'

'You put your weight on your inside foot. Like this,' she demonstrated.

'You are good,' Joy said enviously.

'Well, I was lucky enough to have lessons when I was a child. It was skating or ballet, and I chose skating because I liked the speed.'

'Not because you liked all the boys who went skating, of course?' Joy said teasingly.

'Certainly not,' Gemma laughed, and took her arm to show her how to do the turn.

They continued for a while longer, but Joy kept glancing towards the village, eventually saying, 'I think I'll have a rest for a few minutes, Gemma. I'm starting to find I've got muscles I didn't know about! I'll go and sit on one of the benches. No, don't come with me, I know it must be boring trying to teach me, so why don't you go round by yourself for a while? Show me how good I'll be after a few more lessons.'

Gemma demurred, but really wasn't reluctant to skate by herself. All her old skills soon came back and she even tried a few spins and easy jumps. She was skating fast down the length of the lake, weaving her way between the slower groups of people, when she saw a figure in a black and red ski-suit cutting across the lake towards her. She recognised who it was at once and immediately dug in her skates to spin her round, a shower of ice-particles spurting up from the blades, and started to skate swiftly away, praying that Paul hadn't seen her. Her hair blowing out behind her, she zipped along the ice as fast as she dared, her eyes searching the benches for Joy, but the next minute Paul had overtaken her and swung round to halt a couple of yards away from her, putting out his arms to stop her in case she swerved to avoid him.

But as soon as he appeared in front of her, Gemma came to a dead stop. She stood quite still, her face almost as white as the snow, her only movement the rise and fall of her chest as she recovered her breath. Paul slowly lowered his arms and gazed at her for a long moment. He was in better shape than she was and his headlong dash across the ice had hardly even quickened his breathing. His eyes, as they held hers, seemed almost hypnotic and she was unable to look away.

'Why didn't you phone me?' His voice, hard and sharp, broke the spell.

Gemma blinked and looked away. 'You—you told me to get out of your life, remember?'

In one swift movement he crossed the gap between them and put his hand on her arms, gripping so tightly that she could feel it through her clothes. 'No, Gemma, I told you to go home and grow up. All right, I was angry—*mon dieu*, I had cause enough—but I never intended it to be over between us.'

Gemma backed away from him, putting up her arms to push his hands away. 'That wasn't the impression I got,' she said coldly. 'You made it plain enough at the time that you weren't interested in anyone who wasn't willing to—follow through, was the expression you used, I believe.'

'That isn't true and you know it,' Paul replied forcefully. 'Right from the start I let you set the terms, because I was willing to wait until you were ready, until you cared enough to give yourself to me. I thought you were different from the kind of girl that hangs around these resorts and who's willing to go to bed with a man almost as soon as she meets him. The way you held me off and didn't seem to care who I was or how much money I had, all seemed to point towards that. I felt that you would have to care about a man before you let him make love to you. And I was willing to go along with that; I didn't want to rush you or force you into a relationship you weren't ready for.'

Gemma stared miserably down at her boots, unable to look at him. 'But after that night, you can't possibly want to ...?'

'To take up where we left off? I assure you I do. I'll admit that you really threw me that night. You seemed to know so many little ploys that were aimed at rousing me, that for a while I thought you must have been holding out on me, that you were a ... one of the other kind of girls after all, but a cleverer one who'd known how to play hard to get—until you thought there was some opposition around.' He lifted his hands to take hold of hers, but dropped them immediately when she flinched away.

His jaw tightened, but he went on firmly, 'It wasn't until you called a halt to things that I realised I'd been right about you all along, and that you'd only been flirting, testing your powers as a woman. But I'd taken you up on it so quickly that things had got out of hand, and either you were too inexperienced to know when and how to stop me—or because you weren't altogether sure you wanted me to stop.' His voice softened. 'A dangerous game, *chérie*, to play with any man.'

'I—I know. I'm sorry, Paul. I behaved like a fool.'

He lifted her chin so she had to look at him. To her surprise he was smiling. 'Yes, you did. And I shall probably never forgive you, especially for not giving me your address so that I could put things right between us the next day. I've been searching Zermatt for you ever since, the slopes and lifts during the day, the discos and restaurants at night. I thought I'd found you once, but it was someone else.' He felt her jump and stooped to take hold of her hands as he said earnestly, 'Gemma, you don't have to be afraid, I won't force you into anything you're not ready for. But I believe we had something good going for us. I still do.'

Unhappily Gemma tried to pull away from him, but this time he wouldn't let go. 'Paul, I—I can't. It's not just what happened between us,' she added hurriedly when he seemed about to speak. 'It's—you don't know me. We're poles apart. It just wouldn't work.' Desperately she tried to convince him, knowing that it would be wrong to go on deceiving him.

His hands tightened on hers. 'Perhaps not. But let's give ourselves the chance to find out, shall we? Forget that night. We were having fun together before, enjoying each other's company. We can go on doing that. There won't be any commitments on either side. We'll both be free to end it, to just say goodbye and walk away whenever we want to. Will you come out with me again on those terms? Will you, Gemma?'

Mouth trembling, Gemma gazed up at him. She ought to end it now, to say no and go back to England at once. Her lips formed the word but she couldn't say it. The thought of never seeing him again suddenly seemed intolerable. And it would be all right, he had said there would be no commitments between them. She could spend the rest of the holiday just enjoying being with him and then she would be free to go, to resume her own life.

'This is crazy,' she faltered.

'I know, life is crazy. Will you, Gemma?' His eyes looked searchingly into hers.

She gave a trembling sigh. 'All right, if that's what you want?'

'Oh, yes, it's what I want.' He grinned suddenly. 'And this time you're going to tell me where you're staying, I'm not going to let you run away from me again and not know where to find you.' He put his arm round her waist and began to skate along with her while he memorised the address of the chalet, and it was only when he complimented her on her ability that Gemma remembered about Joy. Guiltily she looked along the benches and round the lake, but could see no sign of her friend's familiar figure in her yellow anorak. She realised that Joy must have seen her with Paul and given up waiting. Probably she'd gone to find the others and warn them, or else tell them that their precious experiment was on again, she thought wryly. She stopped suddenly and turned to Paul.

'Paul, how did you find me? You said you usually looked for me by the lifts?'

'Yes, and I intended to today, but as I was leaving the hotel I had a stroke of luck. There were two girls there and I heard one ask, "Where's Gemma?" and the other told her you were here. As they were English and yours is such an unusual name, I took a chance on it being you and came straight down here.'

Gemma's eyes widened. 'Was one a tall girl with glasses and the other shorter and wearing a blue anorak?'

'I think so, I didn't take that much notice. But yes, now I recall the taller girl definitely had on a pair of those large-lensed spectacles.'

Her mouth tightened and for a moment Gemma looked murderous. 'They fixed this! They set the whole thing up in the hope that we'd get back together. Just wait till I get hold of them. Of all the mean tricks!' She looked at Paul and to her annoyance found that he was laughing. 'It's not funny!' she snapped. 'They're supposed to be my *friends*.'

'And they are, whether you admit it or not, very good friends. After all, they *did* get us back together.' His arm tightened round her waist and he pulled her to him, a curious light in his eyes. 'And I wonder just why they thought we needed to be together again. Could it have been something *you* said, or did you perhaps let them see that you were missing me just a little?' His face was very close, his eyes intent.

'Paul, I....' She tried to contradict him but couldn't, and blushed like a schoolgirl.

'Gemma, I know we're in a public place, but I intend to kiss you anyway.' And he did, so expertly that soon Gemma couldn't have cared less if the whole of Zermatt had turned out to watch.

If the realisation that there was only a short time left of their holiday crossed Gemma's mind during the next few days, she pushed it firmly aside. Just like she refused to face the fact that she was deceiving Paul every minute that she was with him. And he seemed to want her to spend all her time with him, coming to pick her up soon after breakfast and only bringing her back so that she could change to go out again in the evenings. Sometimes she felt as if she was riding on a snowball that was rolling down a hill and gradually getting bigger and bigger; she knew that one day the snow would melt away and leave her high and dry, but right now she was willing to just enjoy the ride.

And Paul made it so easy to enjoy. He took her hang-gliding again and patiently helped her to improve her skiing, taking her to a quiet spot on the mountain to do so. He seemed to like to get away from the crowds, to be alone with her, and twice he drove her out of Zermatt to a much smaller village with hardly any modern hotels and where the mountains were so close that the towering peaks and glaciers seemed to hang in the sky above them.

In the evenings they would drive to quiet, candlelit restaurants, but one day when he brought her back in the afternoon it was snowing and Paul suggested they have dinner in his chalet. He looked at her rather quizzically as he did so, and when she didn't answer at once said wryly, 'But I expect you'd prefer to eat in the hotel dining-room. I'll order a table.'

'No, don't do that.' Gemma reached out and touched his hand. 'I—I'd like to have dinner in your chalet.' His fingers closed over hers and she smiled rather shyly at him. 'Don't bother to come for me yourself, just send the sleigh.'

It was still snowing later and there were flakes of it on the fur hood of her coat when Paul opened the door to her. Laughingly he helped her to shake them off and then led her to the great fire to warm herself. If the memory of the last time they had been together before that fire was as alive in his memory as it was in hers, he didn't show it. He merely brought her a drink and told her an amusing anecdote about one of the well-known people who were staying at the hotel.

'It seems he's giving a big party tomorrow night and everyone that he thinks is someone is invited.'

'Are you going?' Gemma asked him as she sipped her drink.

'Not unless you want to.'

'Me? I haven't been invited.'

'It doesn't matter, I'll take you with me if you want to go.'

For a moment Gemma was at a loss; she seemed to remember from Angie's print-out that Paul liked parties and often gave them himself, but she found suddenly that she didn't want to be with him in a big crowd, especially one where people knew him and would probably speculate and gossip about their relationship. She shook her head. 'No thanks. But if you want to go, please don't think that you have to....'

His finger came up to her lips to stop her. 'I don't want to. That's what I was hoping you'd say.'

Dinner was served by a quietly efficient manservant at a table by the huge window, a table that had had several leaves removed so that it was small enough for them to eat in the intimate closeness of candlelight and for Paul's hand to reach out to cover hers often as they talked. The curtains weren't yet closed and high up near Rifflelberg Gemma thought she could make out some pinpoints of light. Paul turned his head to look when she pointed them out.

'I expect they're rehearsing for the torchlight procession,' he remarked casually.

'A torchlight procession? Really? When?' Gemma asked eagerly.

'In a few days' time, I think. Haven't you seen one before?'

'No. Oh, Paul, could we watch it?'

'Of course. We could take part in it, if you like.'

'Oh, could we? I'd love that.' Her eyes sparkled with excitement and he smiled at her indulgently.

'You're like a child who's been promised a treat.'

The eagerness died out of her face and she looked away, not finding a great deal to say for the rest of the meal. Afterwards the manservant discreetly withdrew and Paul suggested they take their liqueurs over to the fire. Gemma did so without demur but sat some distance away from him on the sofa, sipping her drink and gazing rather contemplatively into the flames.

Paul watched her for a while, a frown between his brows, then said softly, 'Gemma, won't you tell me what's the matter?'

She looked steadily down at her drink, running her finger round the rim of the glass until she realised what she was doing and stopped hastily. 'Nothing's the matter. Why should there be?'

'Something that I said must have upset you. Won't you tell me what it was?'

For a moment she didn't answer, then said slowly, 'I suppose I must seem very childish to you?'

Quickly he put down his drink and came to sit close beside her, putting her glass on the floor and turning her to face him. 'No, not childish. Just very young and innocent. Still able to look at the world and find it a new and wonderful place to be alive in. A quality I hope you'll never lose. I don't ever want you to become so blasée and sophisticated that life becomes dull and unexciting.'

Paul was looking at her earnestly, but he made no move to touch her, and Gemma realised that he was deliberately holding back because of where they were, so that left only one thing to do. Without stopping to think about it, she put her arms round his neck and lifted her head to kiss him. He responded warmly but let her keep the mastery, let her take his mouth and discover the delights of touching his lips with tiny exploring kisses, of letting the tip of her tongue meet his. And when she at last moved away her breathing was as ragged as his. He made a move to take her in his arms again, but Gemma decided that might be dangerous. Hastily she changed the subject.

'Don't you like parties?'

Paul looked at her quizzically for a moment, then grinned and let her get away with it. He smoothed back his hair and reached for a cigarette. 'Sometimes, but not the type where people are only invited for their social position and everyone gets drunk on champagne. I used to enjoy them once, I suppose, but they begin to pall when you go to one every other night of the week.'

His voice had become hard and cynical and Gemma felt an urgent need to dispel it. 'My, my,' she said pertly, 'now who's being blasé and sophisticated?'

Bunching his hand into a fist, Paul hit her lightly on the chin before putting his arm round her and gather-

ing her to him. 'You may not believe it, *ma petite*, but
I too was once young and eager.'

Gemma leaned her head on his shoulder, her feet
tucked under her. 'What happened?' she asked softly
as she ran her fingers lightly over the silk of his lapel.
For a long time he didn't speak and she thought that he
wasn't going to answer, that she had invaded too far
into his privacy. He had told her very little about himself and she had never felt close enough to him to ask
before.

But at length he said, 'I think I told you that my
parents split up when I was very young. Naturally I
was taken to live with my mother, but there was a great
deal of bitterness between them and my mother tried to
instil this into me to make me hate my father.' He
paused and Gemma could only guess at the effort it
must cost him to even talk about it. She made a little
movement as if to stop him, but his arms tightened
around her and she was still.

'It wasn't a very pleasant childhood; my mother trying to kill all the natural affection and respect I felt for
my father, and he questioning me every time I saw him,
trying to find out what she'd been saying about him and
in turn trying to poison my mind against her. They
used me to try and get back at each other. Several times
I couldn't stand it and ran away, but I was always taken
back and got a reputation for being wild because of it.
In the end I was sent away to school and that was better—there were only the holidays to be got through. My
father couldn't marry again because my mother refused
to give him a divorce, so I was his sole heir, but he was
so afraid I'd been brainwashed by my mother and
would just hand all his money to her that he refused to
let me learn anything about the business empire I was
due to inherit.' His voice became hard and bitter with
remembered hurt. 'Instead he gave me only a small

allowance but paid for everything I wanted, first when I went to the Sorbonne and afterwards when I began to mix with the so-called jet-set. Cars, boats, holidays, clothes; I had only to send him the bills and he settled them.' His tone was heavy with cynicism. 'I was very lucky, he gave me everything I wanted.'

Except love, except the one thing he needed, Gemma thought, her heart torn for him. 'Oh, Paul!' She reached out to touch his hand, but he stood up abruptly.

Roughly he said, 'Don't pity me, Gemma.'

'I don't, you don't need it. I just feel angry that they could be so unfeeling, so cruel to you when you were a little boy.'

He smiled suddenly and sat down beside her again, taking her hand in his and playing with her fingers. 'The little boy soon grew up and learned how to take care of himself, I assure you.'

'Are your parents still alive?'

'My mother is, but my father died nearly ten years ago and she remarried and went to live in America. I haven't seen her for several years.'

'So you took over his business affairs, after all?'

'Technically I did, but he'd so arranged everything that I wasn't anything but nominally in charge until I was thirty. The whole thing more or less ran itself and I was merely required to sign papers occasionally.' He shrugged. 'And when it became legally mine, nearly three years ago, there didn't seem to be much point in changing the arrangement. I'd got used to the life I was living and there seemed nothing much worth working or striving for—then.'

He changed the subject then and soon afterwards took her home, but from that night Gemma felt more at ease with him; he was no longer a rich, enigmatic stranger, but a man who had fought alone to curb a hard core of bitterness inside him, a fight she wasn't sure that he had yet won completely.

It was two days later when she finally realised that she was in love with him. It happened quite suddenly and unexpectedly. They had driven over to watch the Olympic bobsleigh teams practising and Paul had met some people he knew who were in the French team. One of them offered to give him a ride in a two-man bob and he immediately accepted. Gemma waited at the bottom and watched as the bob rocketed down the high-banked course of packed ice, reaching fantastic speeds as it screamed round the steep curves. It moved faster as it came nearer the bottom, but here also were the worst bends. As she watched in horror, she saw the bob suddenly rise sharply above the rim of the bank, seem to hang perilously in the air for a moment and then crash back down on to the course out of sight. For a moment her whole being was suspended by shock, she couldn't think, couldn't feel, couldn't breathe. Only when the bob came in sight the right way up, the men apparently unharmed, did she start to function again. She felt a great choking sensation of relief that turned to rage as Paul took off his crash helmet and strolled casually towards her.

Rounding on him in a fury, she yelled, 'You big fool! You could have been killed! If that bobsleigh had turned over you would have broken your neck. Well, okay, if that's what you want—it's your neck! But I don't have to stand here and watch you.'

Angrily she turned and hurried away, but Paul caught her up and pulled her close into his arms. *'Doucement, ma petite, doucement!'*

She had been trembling with emotion, but suddenly she became very still and then slowly lifted her head to gaze at him in dawning wonderment. He didn't speak,

but there was a curious air of triumph in the dark eyes
that looked into hers.

The next day Paul had to go to Berne, travelling by
helicopter, but he kept his promise to be back in time
to take her to the torchlight procession. They joined
the laughing crowd of people waiting for the train to
take them up the mountain and when it came Paul
used his broad shoulders to get them into the first car-
riage, but it was so crowded that Gemma was wedged
hard against him, which he didn't seem to mind at all,
in fact putting his arm round her and drawing her even
closer, his eyes looking mockingly down into hers.
Everyone was in infectious good spirits and they
laughed a lot that night. Several people who were only
going to watch got out at Riffelalp, but Paul and
Gemma went on another two stations to Rotenboden
above the nursery slopes. There were several men and
women from Zermatt taking part, and as the train went
on up through the dark of the mountains they started
to sing, and soon everyone was joining in the easy chorus
whether they understood the words or not. They went
on singing even after they had left the train and were
putting on their skis and lining up for the procession.
It was strange to be on the mountain at night; it seemed
totally alien and unfriendly until Gemma looked down
into the valley and saw the lights of Zermatt twink-
ling far below. She felt like a lost sailor who suddenly
sees a light burning in a window far away and knows
that safety is nearby.

They were placed quite near the head of the procession and Paul took an as yet unlit torch, but wouldn't
let her have one. For a second she rebelled, but realised
that she wasn't good enough to ski with only one stick
and probably wouldn't have enjoyed herself so much
anyway if she had to worry about a torch. When everyone was ready, those in the lead set off, dipping their

flambeaux into a brazier as they passed it and then lifting their flaming brands high above their heads. They began to sing again as they went, but quietly now, almost like a hymn. Paul's turn came and Gemma fell into place behind him, the torch lighting their way.

Others took their places behind her and they moved fast through the darkness, making great spiralling curves down the mountain for the watchers in the valley below. Glancing back, Gemma saw the long snakelike column curving out behind her and was suddenly filled with a surging sense of exhilaration. She forgot everything but the total happiness of being here, of being in love for the very first time in her life. It was a moment she would never forget, a moment she would treasure for the rest of her days.

They were well down the mountain now, travelling parallel to the railway, and soon they reached the line of trees which they would skirt before making a deep bend that would take them down the valley that led directly into Zermatt. When they had gone a few hundred yards past the trees, Paul called her name and skied away from the procession, Gemma following. He stopped under the branches of a large fir tree and stuck his torch into the snow.

'What is it?' Gemma asked him in surprise.

'Nothing. Let's watch for a while.'

He put his arm across her shoulders and together they stood and watched the column go past, the dark figures haloed by flickering torches against the pure whiteness of the snow, their voices echoing softly through the mountains. The trees hid them from view for a moment, they appeared again much lower down as they went through a clearing, and then they were gone, leaving them alone on the silent, moonlit mountain. Neither of them moved for several minutes and then

Paul slowly turned her round to face him.

'Why, Gemma, you're crying!'

'I know, isn't it silly? But it was so beautiful. The most beautiful thing I've ever seen.'

'Oh, Gemma, my love. My dearest girl.' He raised his fingers to wipe away her tears and then his hands gripped her shoulders convulsively. '*Je t'aime*. Oh, Gemma, I love you.'

The tears flowed unheeded down her cheeks and slowly, wonderingly she raised her hands to touch his face. 'And I love you. So much, so very much!'

He tried to take her in his arms, but their skis got in the way and he swore softly. 'Damn these skis! I hadn't intended to tell you here, but to wait till later. How can a man possibly do justice to a situation like this when he's hampered by skis?'

Gemma laughed shakily. 'Then shall we get off this mountain and find somewhere where you *can* do justice to it?'

'Now that, *ma mie*, is a very good idea.' He laughed, a strong, masculine laugh of pure happiness that went ringing round the mountains. Then he picked up the torch to guide them down the valley in the track of the procession. A lone torch far, far behind the others.

When they reached Paul's chalet he immediately took her in his arms, kissing her passionately, letting her know just how much she meant to him, and it was a long time before he let her go.

'You'd better take off that ski-suit, you'll feel the cold when you go home if you don't,' he said huskily.

Gemma put her head to one side. 'That *almost* sounds like a line you've used before,' she said teasingly.

He grinned. 'Wouldn't you like to know?'

He went quickly up the stairs to his room to change into casual slacks and silk polo-neck shirt, and when he came back Gemma had taken off her padded suit and was wearing only a very long sweater that came down over her hips and a pair of thick tights, with over them a pair of gaily-coloured, knitted leg-warmers with all the toes sewn in individually.

Paul laughed openly when he saw the latter. 'I always wondered what you girls wore under your suits.'

'Well, now you know. As if you didn't before. I bet you've had dozens of girls stripping off for you in front of that fire.' She put her arms round his neck and stood on tiptoe to bite his ear gently.

'Mm, thousands,' he agreed as he kissed her neck. 'Does it matter?'

'No.' Her lips moved around to explore his jawline. 'Nothing matters except that you said you loved me.'

'Oh, *mon ange. Je t'adore!*' His lips found hers bruisingly, forcing them apart and kissing her with a fierce desire that left her feeling weak and giddy.

'Oh, Paul!' She clung to him, feeling his heart hammering in his chest. Presently she drew away a little and looked down at her toes before saying falteringly, 'Does this mean that we can go to bed together?'

His hands gripped her arms tightly. 'Do you want to?'

Slowly, huskily, she said, 'Yes, I want to.'

'And so do I. More than you'll ever even begin to understand.' He reached down and tilted her face up to look at him. 'But we're not going to. Not until after we're married. I want you to come to me on our wedding night with the most precious gift that a woman can ever give to a man.'

Gemma's eyes widened and a look of fear came into them. 'Married? But—but we can't get married. Paul, you don't understand. We don't live the same kind of life. It wouldn't work!' Her voice rose in a panic and she tried to draw away, but he caught her wrists and held them.

Tensely he said, 'Gemma, back there on the mountain you said you loved me. Did you mean it?'

Her voice was now little more than an unhappy whisper. 'Yes. You know I did.'

'Then that's all that matters. I want you for my wife, nothing less. And we'll work it out, because I've never in my life wanted anything so much as I want to make you happy.' He pulled her close against him, her head buried in his shoulder, holding her so tightly that he hurt her. 'Oh, Gemma, you're all I want. Without you there's nothing.' But presently he let her go and said huskily, 'Look, this is why I went to Berne today. I went to collect this.' He took a small leather box from his pocket and opened it. Inside there was a ring. An engagement ring. It was in platinum with three fine diamonds set in a geometric design, and was very beautiful.

Slowly she raised her eyes to his. 'To collect it?'

'Yes, I ordered it soon after we started going out together.'

Her lashes came down over her eyes. 'You were very sure of me, then?'

'No, only very sure of myself. I fell in love with you the day I nearly lost you down the crevasse. I knew then just how much you meant to me and I just hoped and prayed that you would eventually feel the same way. And you did, although I almost had to kill myself to make you realise it.'

There was laughter in his voice now and Gemma looked quickly up at him. 'When you nearly crashed on the bobsleigh? You knew?'

'Of course. A woman never yells at a man like that unless she cares about him. So I knew it was time for me to go to Berne to collect the ring.' He took hold of her left hand and slid the jewel on to her third finger. 'So say you'll marry me, Gemma, and make me the happiest man in the world tonight.'

The snowball had grown out of all proportion, she

knew that she ought to jump off now before it consumed her, but she couldn't. Nothing seemed to matter
except the love she saw in his eyes and the longing in
her own heart.

Her eyes were wet with tears as she said, 'Oh, Paul,
I love you. Promise me that no matter what happens,
you'll always remember that I loved you.' And then she
was in his arms, oblivious to everything but the need
to be near him.

CHAPTER EIGHT

It was the early hours of the morning before Paul took Gemma home and kissed her a lingering farewell in the shadowed doorway of the Chalet Domino. But there were many parties being celebrated in Zermatt that night and the other girls weren't home; she strongly suspected that their party would turn out to be an all-night affair and they probably wouldn't turn up until after breakfast.

Slowly Gemma unzipped her ski-suit and took off her boots. The fire had died right down, but she poked it and put on some logs and soon it began to flicker into life again. Sitting down on the hearthrug, she leaned her back against an armchair and gazed into the weak flames. It seemed to have been a night of fire and flame today; first the torches borne by the skiers and then the huge log fire in Paul's chalet, by whose light he had made love to her, taking off her sweater to kiss and caress her so expertly and passionately that she had moaned in ecstasy and longed for him to take her now —now! 'Soon, my heart, soon,' he had whispered, and held her quivering body tight against his. And then home, back to this poor imitation of the fire he had lit within her.

For a long time she just sat, her hands folded across her breasts, almost as if holding the memory of his love-making to her, but at last she brought her mind back to reality with reluctant dread. She didn't want to; she would much rather have stayed forever in a state of suspension where only tonight was real. But tomorrow had to be faced, had to be lived through, as she had known it must. This last week, ever since she had got back with Paul, she had been living in a fool's paradise, a self-induced state where she had put all thoughts of the future and the consequences of her actions firmly aside. Tomorrow could take care of itself, she had lived only for today and the intoxicating happiness of the present.

But now tomorrow was here, just a few hours away, and she had to face the hardest task of her young life. Gemma glanced down at the ring and slowly turned it on her finger. If Paul hadn't proposed, if he hadn't wanted to marry her, it would all have been so easy. She could have said, 'Goodbye, my holiday's over. It's been fun,' and just walked out of his life, have been just another holiday romance. How she would have found the courage to do it without letting him find out that she loved him, she didn't quite know, but she would have managed it somehow. But now—now everything was different. He had refused to take no for an answer, and whatever she did, she was going to hurt him, and she didn't know if she could bear it. The Paul Verignac she had fallen in love with had turned out to be a very different man than they had first supposed him from their research. A rich playboy, perhaps, but one who was essentially a lonely and embittered man, one who had sometimes used women as he had been used, but who was capable of deep and unselfish love. A love she was going to have to throw back in his face to make him even more bitter and vindictive.

Gemma put her face in her hands in utter misery. There was no way she could soften the blow. Some mad urgency within her that was greater than any sane and sensible feelings had led her headlong down a path that was going to bring nothing but unhappiness to both of them. And the only way she could think of that might help him a little, might make it possible for him to purge himself of her and eventually fall in love with someone else, was to make her part in the conspiracy even blacker than it was, to make him so disgusted with her that he would hate and despise her. It was a long time before the battle between her longing for him not to think too badly of her and the inner knowledge of what she had to do, was over. At least she could do this for him. And by punishing herself she might atone a little for what she was about to do to Paul.

Her limbs felt stiff when she at last rose from the rug. The fire had gone out long ago and she shivered. Then deliberately she straightened and ran upstairs. Quickly she removed the disguise and went into Angie's room. All the typewritten notes on the experiment were in a neat stack on a table beside the typewriter. Taking the cover off the machine, Gemma inserted a fresh sheet of paper and began to type a new set of notes. Essentially she kept them the same, but left out her own reluctance to take part, and from the time she started going out with Paul described his reactions far more and made her own actions appear very calculated and deliberate as she put in even the full details of his attempts to make love to her. It took a great deal of agony to describe the incidents of that night in cold-blooded clinical terms, and by the time she came to the last sentence the tears were running down her cheeks. Angrily she brushed them away. She had to do this, she had to!

'The experiment has, therefore, been a complete success,' she typed. 'And it is the findings of those taking part that if sufficient information can be gathered about the subject it is possible to contrive the necessary circumstances and emotions required to lead to the desired result, i.e. marriage.'

She sat back and took the sheet from the typewriter. A tear fell on it as she stapled it to the others. It wasn't

very good, she knew; she had had no time to think it
out and she could only hope that it would be convinc-
ing. Tiredly she stood up and drew back the curtains
to look out. The first faint rays of dawn were beginning
to lighten the sky to a pinkish grey that promised a fine,
bright day. The mountains seemed to be slumbering
still, their snow-capped peaks resting before they ex-
posed their dreaming white slopes to the sun. Dully
Gemma wondered how long it would be before she
could look at snow and remember today without this
pain in her heart that was so fierce she thought it would
consume her. Months, perhaps? Years? The rest of her
life? Hastily she took the sheets and the original print-
out and put them into a large folder. This was no time
to think of the future, she still had to get through
the next few hours.

A long shower with the water as hot as she could
bear it revived her a little, and then she went to her
own room to change into travelling clothes. She was
methodically packing the rest of her things when she
heard a sleigh draw up outside and then the whispered,
giggling goodbyes of the others as they took their
leave of their boy-friends.

It was Lisa who saw the light under her door. 'Hi,
Gemma, did you have a good time?' The other girl
started as she came into the room, and then stopped
short as she saw the open suitcases on Gemma's bed.
'Are you packing already? We have two more days yet
—three if you count today.'

'I've decided to go back ahead of you,' Gemma answered, her voice admirably steady in the circumstances.

Lisa's voice was sharp. 'You haven't had bad news
from home, have you?'

'No, nothing like that. I've just had enough of Zermatt, that's all.'

'Gemma, don't try to fool me—I can read you like a book. Tell me what's happened.'

Lisa's raised voice had brought the others to her room and they crowded in, Joy yawning sleepily. 'What's the matter?'

'It's Gemma, she's running away from something.'

Gemma smiled thinly. 'Not running away, just making a strategic withdrawal.'

'A withdrawal from what?' Lisa asked, then added impatiently, 'Gemma, will you please stop packing and tell us what's happened?'

Slowly Gemma turned to them, her eyes shadowed by unhappiness. 'All right, I'll tell you. You had reason to celebrate tonight. Because your experiment has been a success. A magnificent, resounding success! Angie will be the computer queen of Oxford when she gets back and tells them all about it. Yes, that's right,' she went on as she saw their amazed faces, 'tonight Paul Verignac proposed to me. He actually asked me to be his wife! Look, he even ordered a ring to be specially made for me. None of your antique second-hand stuff for Paul Verignac. Only the newest and the best is good enough for the girl he wants to marry!' Despite herself her voice faltered and she broke off, biting her lip.

'Wow!' Joy was staring at the ring. 'Is that for real?'

Angie sank slowly on to the bed amid the piles of clothes. 'I don't believe it,' she said wonderingly. 'It really worked. It really, really worked!'

Lisa was gazing at Gemma searchingly. 'So why are you leaving?'

'Why?' Gemma's voice filled with despair. 'Because you left something out of your calculations. You left out feelings and emotions. You said that I would be just another woman in his life. Well, it isn't true. Because he fell in love with me—no, not with me, with the creature we created for him. For the first time in

his life he found a woman he wanted to spend the rest
of his life with, and now I have to go to him and tell
him that he only fell in love with a doll, a puppet that
moved whenever a computer pulled the strings. *That's*
what you left out of your calculations!'

The sun was higher in the sky but it was still very
early and most people were still having breakfast when
Gemma raised a trembling hand to knock on the door
of Paul's chalet. The temperature was low enough for
snow, but she hardly felt it, she was too cold and
frightened inside to worry about the weather. She was
wearing the wig but not the lenses, instead a pair of
dark glasses masked her eyes, and under her arm she
carried the folder with the computer print-out and the
notes she had typed. After a few minutes the manservant who had served dinner to them answered the
door.

Gemma was taken aback, she had braced herself for
Paul to answer. 'I—I should like to see Monsieur Verignac, please.'

'I'm afraid Monsieur Verignac has not yet risen,
mademoiselle. If you will come back later.'

The man went to shut the door, but Gemma hastily
stopped him. 'No, please, it's very important. If you'll
just tell him that Miss Kenyon is here, I'm sure he'll
want to see me.'

He looked at her disapprovingly and then shrugged.
'Very well. One moment.' He shut the door again, but
was soon back and spoke far more graciously. 'If you
will come in, mademoiselle, Monsieur Verignac will be
down in only a few minutes.'

He showed her in and then went upstairs again, presumably to valet for Paul. Gemma took one look at
the fireplace and the still dishevelled rugs in front of
it and crossed firmly to the picture window where she
stood gazing out unseeingly. It seemed a lifetime and

yet no time at all before she heard Paul's light step
taking the stairs two at a time and turned to face him.

He was dressed in slim-fitting navy trousers and a
matching silk shirt which was open at the neck to reveal a heavy gold medallion. His hair was still damp
from the shower.

'*Chérie!*' He took her hand in both his and carried
it to his lips, this one gesture when it went with the love
in his eyes a caress that surpassed anything that had
gone before. 'Darling, couldn't you sleep either? Thank
you for coming back to me so quickly. It was hell to be
parted from you even for these few hours. But at least
I could dream of you all night.'

'You said you didn't sleep,' she replied unsteadily
because she couldn't bring herself to say what she had
come to say.

Paul smiled. 'One doesn't have to be asleep to dream.'
He drew her towards the table and she saw that it was
already set. 'Have you had breakfast? I'll tell Anton to
set another place.'

'No, Paul. I have to talk to you,' she said urgently.

'Of course. And I've lots to tell you. Plans I've been
making for our wedding and honeymoon. And we must
go to England so that I can meet your family as soon
as possible. But come and have a cup of coffee first. And
you haven't yet kissed me this morning.' He went to
draw her towards him possessively, his eyes full of pride
and tenderness, but Gemma stepped quickly away from
him.

'I came to return this.' She took off the ring and put
it on the table, not trusting herself to withstand the
touch of his hand.

To her dismay he laughed. 'Oh, Gemma, have you
had second thoughts already? Now why don't you take
off those glasses and let me kiss you? I guarantee all

your doubts and fears will fly out of the window just as soon as I do.'

With a shaking hand Gemma reached up and took off the glasses. 'All right, they've served their purpose. And so has this.' She lifted off the wig and shook her head to let her hair fall free. Slowly she lifted her eyes to find him staring at her in a shattering silence.

His voice grown suddenly tight, he said at length, 'So it seems I'm not to marry a blue-eyed blonde after all. Quite a transformation!' His voice dropped and he looked at her searchingly. 'Why, Gemma?'

She took a deep breath and raised her chin determinedly. 'It's all here.' She laid the folder on the table beside the glasses and the heap of blonde hair. 'My friends and I were conducting a scientifically organised experiment.'

Paul raised his brows, a half-amused look in his eyes. 'What for? To see if gentlemen preferred blondes?'

'No, to see if a man could be brought to the point of proposing to a woman when she deliberately set out to make him do so.'

He became very still. 'What did you say?'

Gemma wanted to die, but she forced herself to go on. 'We saw a photograph of you in a magazine back in England and we decided you would do for the purpose of our experiment. So we fed everything we could find about you into a computer: magazine articles, interviews with women you'd had affairs with, that sort of thing, and then came here to find you. To provide the kind of woman you go for and then use the computer findings to see if we could make you fall for her—me,' she amended, her eyes momentarily dark with misery that was quickly hidden. 'And to see if you could be made to—propose marriage. Which you did, of course. And as the others have now seen the ring as proof of the proposal, I've brought it back.'

Her fingers tightened on the back of the chair she was holding and it became increasingly difficult to speak. Fleetingly she raised her eyes to his face and then looked quickly away, her heart hammering. As matter-of-factly as she could, she said, 'You'll find it all in this copy of our notes on the experiment, and I brought you the computer print-out in case you're interested. I'll leave you to your breakfast now. Good morning.'

She hurried down the steps and across the large room, praying that Paul would be too stunned to follow her, but she had only taken a few strides before she heard him move. There was an almost overwhelming urge to run, but she fought it down and turned coolly to face him when he caught her arm and spun her round.

'Oh, no, you don't! You're not walking out of here until you've explained just exactly what you're talking about,' he said savagely, his face white and taut with suppressed emotion.

'I told you,' Gemma replied as calmly as she could. 'It's all in the notes.'

'Are you trying to tell me that you deliberately sought me out? That our whole relationship, right from the very beginning, was nothing but a sham, a deliberate set-up?'

'Yes.'

Slowly he said, 'You promised to marry me, Gemma.'

'No, I didn't, you just took it for granted that I would.' She found that she couldn't bear the anguish in his eyes, so she went back to the table and picked up the sheaf of typewritten notes. 'Here it is, read for yourself.' Flicking over the pages, she came to where they had first arrived in Zermatt and held them out to him.

Slowly he took the sheets from her, his eyes burning into hers, then he lowered them and began to read. His face paled as he turned over the pages, running his eyes down them and reading only parts of it. Gemma could almost tell what he was reading by the tightening of his jaw and the thinness of his mouth. When he came to the end pages he read them and then went back and read them again as if he couldn't believe it. His eyes, when he at length raised his head, were as bleak and cold as the mountains.

'Why me?' When she didn't answer at once he seized her wrist, his fingers biting hard into her flesh. 'Why did you pick on me as the victim of your intellectual charade?'

Gemma shrugged. 'We just happened to come across your photograph and knew that we could get plenty of information about you, that's all. Also we thought it wouldn't do you any harm to be a taught a lesson, to show you that you can be used just like you use women.'

'And did you give no thought to my possible feelings when you began to plot your clever little experiment?'

'We did, but we decided that as you'd had so many women already, one more wouldn't make any difference to you.'

His fingers tightened, digging cruelly into her wrist so that she winced with pain. He smiled thinly.

'So you gave me the kind of woman you thought I wanted—a blue-eyed blonde.' His voice was contemptuous. 'Tell me, Gemma, did you enjoy playing the part?'

She looked away, taking a deep breath before she said as disdainfully as she could, 'No, you're much too superficial.'

At that he swung her forcibly round so that she stumbled and fell back against the wall. He pinned her against it, his face very close so that she could hear the raggedness of his breathing, see the rage and torment in his eyes.

'More than once I've come close to taking you to bed with me. Last night you almost begged me to. So what if I had, Gemma? How would that have worked into your precious report?' he asked savagely.

Grimly she steeled herself to lie to him. 'It was hardly likely. It was obvious from the first that you picked up every girl who came your way and then dropped them when you'd had enough of them, so you were bound to be intrigued by one who held out. And even if you had insisted it wouldn't have mattered to me. One should be willing to make any sacrifice, however unpleasant, in the furtherance of scientific. . . .'

The control he had held over his emotions snapped completely. He began to drag her towards the stairs. 'Damn you, you lying little cheat,' he shouted, 'then we'll see just how willing you are to sacrifice yourself!'

Gemma screamed and fell down the steps to the main room, falling on her knees. Paul pulled her up by her arm and dragged her along by it. The manservant appeared at the top of the stairs and came running down when he saw what was happening, calling Paul's name and trying to pull him away from her. Angrily Paul shook him off like a fly, but the man's intervention had some effect on him because he pulled Gemma to her feet and slammed her back against the newel post. His hands closed tightly around her throat and his eyes were murderous in his ashen face, his voice and breathing uncontrolled.

'Just tell me one thing. Last night on the mountain— you said that you loved me. Was that also a lie?'

Slowly she forced herself to look at him. She tried to speak disdainfully, but found she couldn't and her voice came out in a husky whisper. 'What do you think?'

Paul flinched away from her and seemed to crumple as if she had knifed him in the stomach. Gemma tore herself from his suddenly slack hands and turned to run, the tears starting to stream down her cheeks.

The sleigh was waiting outside and the girls standing anxiously by it. They had wanted to face him with her, but she had insisted on going alone. Lisa hurried to meet her as she ran towards them. She started to say, 'I was almost coming to get you,' when she saw Gemma's face and hurriedly bundled her into the sleigh, already piled with their cases. Angie and Joy jumped in beside them and put their arms round her and rubbed her hands, trying uselessly to comfort her as the sleigh trotted briskly towards the station.

March came in wet and windy. It had been raining incessantly for a week and Gemma hurried home from the library, the skirts of her mac whipping round her legs, her umbrella protecting her only a little from the driving rain. Thankfully she reached the house and ran upstairs to let herself into the apartment. All the lights were on and she could hear Joy banging on the door of the bathroom and yelling at Lisa to hurry.

'Come on, Lisa, I have a date!'

'So have I,' Lisa retorted as she came out, a towel wrapped round her hair. She went to her own room and came out a few minutes later to go into Angie's room. 'Angie, have you got my hair dryer?' There followed a sharp argument until Lisa emerged triumphantly carrying the dryer.

Gemma gave a rather exasperated grin and went into the kitchen to make herself a coffee. The apartment had become bedlam during the last few weeks with the other three hectically trying to get ready for dates and then dashing out at the last minute. It had started nearly three weeks ago when Angie had met an American computer expert who had come to Oxford to study their computer system. Then Lisa and Joy had got into a friendly argument with two men they met at the debating society and they had got friendlier as the argument progressed into a nearby pub. Since then one or other of them seemed to have a date nearly every night and, today being Saturday, they were all going out.

Which was why Gemma had gone to the library to collect some books she needed for her studies; it was going to be a long evening here alone and she would need something to keep her occupied. Not that she would be able to keep her mind on her work for very long. Since their hasty return from Zermatt she had found her mind wandering away from her studies time and time again. She had never known that unhappiness could be like this. The sense of desolation that came over her whenever she thought of Paul was so physical that she could hardly bear it. Why did an emotional pain become something physical, turn into a positive ache—heartache? She had hurt him and she hated herself for it. She had thought that work would prove to be a panacea and she had thrown herself into it, but she had only to read a love poem and her thoughts would fly back to the mountains, her mind filled with the sweetest memories that left her staring blankly at the page until reality forced its way into her senses and she returned reluctantly to the aching emptiness of the present.

Slowly she filled the percolator and carried it into the living-room, plugging it in and standing it on a small coffee table by the armchair near the fire. Going back to the kitchen she made herself a sandwich and then settled down in the armchair, a book open on her lap and notepad and pen beside her. When Angie came into the room wearing the black dress Gemma had worn in Zermatt—without the panels sewn back on, Gemma noticed in wry amusement—she was already immersed in her work.

Angie looked at her in some concern. 'Gemma, why don't you come out with us tonight? I'll phone Steve and tell him to bring a friend along. Or you could bring someone to make a four, if you'd rather. You went out with that new don at St John's several times before,' she paused awkwardly, 'before Christmas; why not ring him? He asked me only this week what had happened to you.'

'Did he? What did you tell him?'

Angie shrugged slightly. 'Only that you got stuck on someone you'd met on holiday and hadn't got over it yet. And you won't get over him if you stay here alone every night, moping.'

'I'm not moping, I'm studying, and so should you be if you want to pass your exams. You only have a couple of months left, you know,' Gemma pointed out.

Angie raised her eyes to heaven. 'Don't tell me, I know.' She sat in the other armchair, her legs dangling over the arm. 'But I've never met anyone like Steve before. We're really on the same wavelength. And he's helped me a lot with my work, explaining American ideas for future computer functions that I didn't even know existed. And he was terrifically interested when I told him about our experiment.'

Gemma looked at her sharply. 'You told him about it?'

'Oh, don't worry, he doesn't know who took part. I didn't tell him your name, and Paul Verignac is just referred to as Mr X in my notes.'

'You let him read them?'

'Yes, I lent them to him. He promised to give them back to me tonight.'

There was a little frown of worry between Gemma's brows as she took this in, but then she dismissed it. What harm could it do so long as no one knew that Paul had been involved? It was all over now; dead and done with.

Angie went on trying to persuade her to go out and Lisa and Joy added their voices when they were ready, so Gemma was almost pleased when their various boy-friends arrived and whisked them away, leaving her in peace and quiet. She tried to settle back to her work, but shifted restlessly in her chair, unable to concentrate. She decided to make herself another coffee, so switched on the percolator and took her cup into the kitchen to rinse. The door of the cooker had been left partly open and as she went to shut it she noticed how filthy it was. Impulsively she decided to clean it there and then, putting on a plastic apron over her sweater and jeans and tying a scarf gipsy-fashion over her hair.

Soon she was on her knees in front of the oven, a long smear of dirt on her cheek where she had pushed her hair out of her eyes. It was easier when she had something physical to do, for a little while she could forget, and perhaps using up her energy might make her sleep tonight instead of lying awake for hours, her mind a welter of unhappiness. But she had hardly got started before the doorbell rang. Gemma gave an exasperated sigh and sat back on her heels, half toying with the idea of not answering it; friends dropping in for a drink and a chat were the last thing she wanted tonight. The bell rang again, imperatively, and she realised that the light from the kitchen could be seen through the glass panels of the front door. Reluctantly she stood up and pulled off her rubber gloves and apron. Grumbling a little to herself, she went to answer it just as the bell rang for the third time. Annoyed, she pulled open the door in some haste, prepared to rebuke the noisy caller—but nothing came out. She just stood with her mouth open, staring.

Paul was leaning his broad shoulders casually against the door jamb, the collar of his trench-coat turned up against the rain. His eyes dropped down her slender young body in insolent appraisal and there was an acid twist at the corner of his mouth. He seemed to expect her to speak, but she just stood there staring at him numbly, knowing that if she let go of the door her legs wouldn't support her. After a minute longer he stepped past her into the hall and then waited to let her close the door. But she still stood as though frozen, only her eyes, wide and frightened, following his movements. Impatiently he thrust the door shut himself and she retreated precipitately down the hallway as he came towards her. As she neared the bathroom door she looked quickly round, a wild idea of locking herself in there going through her head.

'If you try it,' Paul said menacingly, 'I'll kick the door down.'

One look at his set face showed her that he meant it. Heart pounding, she preceded him into the living-room and then turned to face him. 'What are you doing here? What do you want?'

Paul unhurriedly unbelted his coat and dropped it on a chair before he answered. 'You and I have some talking to do.' He said it quite calmly, but there was a distinctly unpleasant note in his voice.

Bravely Gemma tried to match his coolness. 'We said everything there was to say back in Zermatt.'

'On the contrary, I thought of quite a few things I wanted to say to you after you took off, especially when I'd read through those notes you so kindly left behind,' he added with acid irony.

Gemma licked lips that had suddenly gone dry. 'How —how did you find me?'

He sat down in the armchair she'd been using, his long legs stretched casually out in front of him, his fingers pyramided together as he looked at her over the top of them. 'It was really very simple,' he told her mockingly. 'I got your friend's home address from the agency from whom you'd hired the Chalet Domino. A phone call to her home gave me this address. The agency weren't supposed to disclose it, of course, but it's amazing what a little money can do in the right quarter, as you found out with my driver,' he added sneeringly.

'Then you must also know that I share this apartment with friends. They're out at the moment but I'm expecting them back shortly, so I'd advise you to leave at once.'

To her consternation, Paul gave an exaggerated smile and began to slowly applaud her. '*Très bien*. I had almost forgotten what a good actress you are.'

'What—what do you mean?'

'I mean that your friends are now having dinner at a restaurant where they will all have met up—quite by chance, of course—and then one of the men they are with will tell them that he's been invited to a party in a village near Aylesbury and they will all go on there. It will be such a good party that their escorts won't be in a fit state to drive them home, even if they wanted to leave. So—we'll have all night for our little talk,' he paused unpleasantly, '*if* it takes that long.'

Gemma stared at him, her eyes large in a face that was completely drained of colour. 'What are you saying?'

'Oh, I think you know.' He got lightly to his feet and crossed to her with the grace of a wild and dangerous animal. 'After I knew who you all were and where you lived, I did a little investigating of my own—oh, nothing as sophisticated as computers, just an ordinary detective agency—and I found out just what kind of girls your apartment mates were and provided fitting escorts for them. Intellectual ones, of course, for such clever, intelligent graduates. Just like you did for me.' His voice became a sneer. 'They fell for it completely.'

'Just like you did!' Gemma retorted, bright spots of colour appearing high on her cheekbones.

His jaw tightened. 'Just like me,' he agreed.

'You had no right to do that. They didn't hurt you.'

His eyes blazed and he showed anger for the first time. 'I had every right! They were as much a part of the deception as you were.'

'But they like these men. What if they fall....' She broke off abruptly and looked away.

'Exactly,' he said sardonically. 'It would be poetic justice, wouldn't it? A fitting retribution for the way they tried to manipulate me.'

'And me?' Gemma said unsteadily. 'Was I supposed to meet someone too?'

'Oh, no, you're a special case. I've got something far more interesting lined up for you,' he said silkily. For the first time he lifted his hand to touch her, letting his fingers slide down the side of her face and continue down her neck and chest to her breasts.

Angrily she jerked away from him, but not before he had felt the tremor that ran through her body.

'What do you want?'

'Do I really have to spell it out to you?' he jeered. 'I want to possess you sexually. I want to go to bed with you whenever and wherever I feel like it, until I've grown tired of you and have no further use for you. You made some promises back in Zermatt which you didn't keep, and I intend to....'

'No! I didn't promise you anything,' Gemma broke in desperately.

'Perhaps not in so many words, but you certainly implied them with everything else,' he said harshly. 'You owe me, you beautiful little cheat, and I'm going to make sure you pay.' He stood there glaring at her, his anger for the moment held in check but very near the surface, daring her to defy him. 'So you'd better go and start packing. Just bring enough to last you for a few days; you can get anything else you want in Paris.'

'Paris?' She looked bemused.

'Certainly, you don't think I intend to spend our first

night together here, do you? Go and pack,' he ordered.

'No, you can't make me!'

'Oh, yes, I can, Gemma.' He took a hip flask from his pocket and showed it to her. 'All I have to do is make you so drunk you don't know what you're doing. Then I'll put you in my car and take you to the plane I have waiting to fly us to France. You see, it's really very simple. But don't worry,' his eyes ran over her insultingly, 'you'll probably be back here in a few months. It shouldn't take long to grow tired of you.'

'I can't leave here,' Gemma said helplessly. 'I have my exams to do in a few weeks.'

Suddenly, in absolute fury, he seized her and forced her to look into his eyes. Shaking with rage, he shouted, 'Damn your exams! You're going to come with me if I have to knock you senseless!'

Wildly she began to struggle, hitting him with her fists and trying to kick him. As he sought to catch her wrists, she caught him off balance and he fell, taking her with him. They rolled on the floor, still fighting. As he tried to pin her under him with his weight, Gemma flung out her hand to hit him again, but he jerked his head aside and her arm caught the frail coffee table. It wobbled, and almost in slow motion she saw the percolater and its stream of scalding hot liquid start to topple towards her face.

She must have cried out in terror, for the next second Paul's arm had come across to shield her and with the other hand he was dragging her out of the way. She felt his body arch and heard him give a gasp of pain that was quickly bitten off.

'Paul!' She rolled out from under him and saw that he was doubled up in pain. 'Oh, Paul, my darling! Let me see. Let me help you.' She fell to her knees beside him and tried to look at his arm, but he wouldn't let her.

'*C'est rien*. It's nothing.' He tried to turn away.

'Paul, for heaven's sake let me see!'

Something in her voice made him turn his head quickly to look at her and what he saw made him go suddenly slack so that she was able to take his hand gently in hers.

'We must put it under the cold tap quickly.' She hurried him out to the bathroom and helped him to take off his jacket and watch and roll up his sleeve before putting his left hand under the running water. Already the skin was an ugly red colour.

'It isn't as bad as it looks,' he told her. 'Most of the stuff went on my sleeve.'

'I'll—I'll get something to bandage it.'

She went to turn away, but he said quietly, 'Gemma,' and she stopped, her body quivering. Slowly he reached out and turned her round to face him. He saw that she was crying silently, the tears running unheeded down her cheeks.

'Oh, Paul, your hand. Your poor hand!'

'Far better my hand than your lovely face,' he said softly. He lifted his right hand to her neck and drew her gently towards him. 'Your eyes, your cheeks, your mouth.'

There were only a few inches between them now and his eyes were like dark, smouldering fires gazing deeply into hers. With a little sigh, Gemma closed the gap between them. She put her arms round his neck, leaning her head against his shoulder.

His voice sounded strange, unlike him. 'You'll come with me to France?'

'Yes.' It was little more than a whisper, but he heard it quite clearly.

'Give up your exams, everything?'

'Yes.'

His lips sought hers insistently and she raised her

head to return his kiss. At first his lips were soft and gentle but then became firm as they demanded a response, their pressure increasing fiercely, possessively. It was only when she felt something wet on her back that she realised he had taken his burnt hand out of the water, and she drew away from him in concern.

Hurrying away, she came back with the first-aid box and carefully bandaged the burn. His wrist and the back of his hand had taken the worst of it, but luckily his fingers weren't too bad and Gemma was able to leave them uncovered. Eyes averted, she concentrated on her task, although she knew that he was watching her all the time.

'You really ought to see a doctor,' she said worriedly. 'Promise me that you will?'

'First thing in the morning,' he agreed.

'Perhaps you'd better sit down for a while.'

She led the way back into the living-room and Paul sat and watched her while she cleaned up the mess of spilled coffee. When she had finished she hung up his coat and straightened cushions until he said imperatively, 'You're fidgeting. Come here.'

Gemma hesitated and then slowly crossed to stand beside him. He put out his good hand and pulled her down on to his lap, then reached up to untie the scarf round her hair. She could feel the hard muscles of his thighs beneath hers, feel the warmth of his body.

'I—I'd better go and pack,' she said uncertainly.

'Not yet—there's plenty of time.'

He began to stroke her hair very lightly and she gave a long, shuddering sigh. 'Oh, Paul, I'm sorry. I'm so very sorry.'

'For my hand?'

'No, for what we did to you in Zermatt. It was totally irresponsible. Unforgivable.'

'But you didn't want to go along with it. And you

tried to back out before things went too far.'

Gemma looked at him in amazement. 'How did you know that?'

'From the real experiment notes. I instructed Angie's boy-friend to get them for me. Those others you gave to me looked too perfect to have been written up on a day-to-day basis, so I guessed there must have been another set. They made interesting reading. Why did you substitute the others, Gemma?' he asked, watching her closely. 'They damned you utterly.'

'Because—because what happened was entirely my fault. I had every opportunity to tell you the truth and yet I didn't take it. I could have brought everything to a halt when it was still a harmless trick, but I just let it ride until ... until. ...' She was unable to go on.

'Until you realised that I was in love with you?'

She nodded, unable to look at him.

'But why did you take all the blame on yourself, make yourself out to be uncaring?'

'I thought that if I made you hate me it would be easier for you, you'd be able to get over it more quickly,' she explained tiredly. 'I knew that you'd be hurt, but I hoped that. ...' Her voice trailed off. 'I never thought that you'd come after us like this.'

His hand dropped to her arm and gripped tightly. 'Did it never occur to you to stay and marry me anyway?'

She looked at him in some surprise. 'No, I knew you'd want nothing more to do with me after the way we'd tricked you. And anyway, you don't like brunettes. You didn't even recognise me when you saw me as I really was.'

For the first time a glint of amusement came into his eyes, but then he said, 'I'm a very rich man, Gemma, I could have given you everything you wanted.'

A frown came between her brows. 'Money isn't that

important. Okay, it's nice to have, but only if you've gained it because of your own achievements.' Slowly she added, 'The way you live—it's like being a parasite.'

'So you disapproved of me completely; my money, my way of life, my women—and yet you went on seeing me and couldn't bring yourself to tell me the truth. And when you realised that I was serious about you you tried to minimise my hurt by blackening yourself. You even came to face me yourself when you could easily have just walked out of my life or written a letter. Why, Gemma?' he asked softly, his eyes intent.

Agitatedly she tried to get up, but he wouldn't let her. 'You—you know why.'

'Say it,' he said urgently. 'I want to hear you say it.'

'Because I love you. I loved you even when I was trying to make you hate me.'

Paul gave a deep sigh, as if he'd just completed a long ski-run and come safely home. 'That's all I wanted to know.' He pulled her down against his shoulder and held her there, encompassed in his arms, for a long time before he eventually said, 'What career had you intended to take up after you completed your exams?'

'It—it doesn't matter.' Her voice was muffled in his shoulder.

'Tell me.'

'Well, I hoped to get a research fellowship into mediaeval manuscripts at a university or museum.'

'Could you do that in France, in Paris?'

Gemma sat up and looked at him uncertainly. 'I suppose so. But you said that you wanted....' She flushed.

'I know, but I'm afraid it will have to wait for a while. I intend to go back to France to take over the control of my companies. Turn myself into a businessman.' He smiled sardonically. 'Learn how to work for my living.'

'You intend to run them yourself? But why?'

Paul looked at her steadily. 'Because my future wife doesn't approve of parasites, of course. And because now I have something worth working and fighting for.'

Gemma's eyes slowly widened as she stared at him in open-mouthed amazement. 'You—you mean. . . .'

'Yes, of course I do, *petite imbécile*. But just make sure you pass those exams, Gemma, because I shall probably have lost the lot in three months.'

But he couldn't say any more because she was kissing him as if she'd never let him go. The hungry weeks of wanting him, of needing him, were over, and coherent thought dissolved beneath the passion of their embrace. She wanted to mould herself into him, to be a part of him.

It was a long, long time before either of them could do anything but murmur words of love and longing, but at last Gemma asked, 'Did you really come here with the intention of carrying me off to France in a drunken stupor if I resisted you?'

He grinned happily, the cynicism completely gone. 'Of course. Although I was hoping like hell that things would turn out this way once we saw each other again. Oh, I'd probably have kept you as my mistress for a couple of weeks before I made an honest woman of you —just to teach you not to trifle with a man's affections, you understand? But I always knew that I wanted to marry you, Gemma.'

'Even though I'm not a blue-eyed blonde?' she asked teasingly. 'And I'm definitely the sweater and jeans type, I can't sail, and there's nothing mysterious about me at all?'

'Those are great drawbacks, admittedly,' he agreed, but then he let his eyes run over her mockingly. 'But you do have other advantages that I think I could learn to live with.'

Gemma wrinkled her nose at him and bunched her fist to playfully punch him on the jaw.

'I might have known you'd hit a wounded man,' he complained. 'But not so wounded that I can't retaliate.' And he caught her hand to bite gently at the base of her thumb, moving his mouth inwards to kiss her palm.

Gemma lifted his hand and carried it to her cheek, her eyes misty with love and happiness. 'Oh, Paul, I'm so glad you came to find me.'

'But you told me to.'

Her eyes widened in surprise. 'I did? But how?'

'You said to me: "No matter what happens, always remember that I love you". When I came to my senses and remembered that and what had happened between us, I knew I had to find you. I just didn't believe that it had meant nothing to you.'

It was nearly an hour later when they heard the front door crash open and running feet in the hall.

Angie burst in shouting, 'It's all right, Gemma, we're here! We found out what was happening and came to. . . .' She broke off and came to a precipitate standstill in the middle of the room so that Lisa and Joy cannoned into her.

Gemma raised her head and looked over Paul's shoulder at their amazed faces. 'Hi,' she said languidly, and turned back to be kissed again.

'But we came to rescue you from him,' Angie said disbelievingly. 'We thought you were being molested.'

'She doesn't look as if she's being molested to me,' Joy put in.

'Actually, I'd say she was rather enjoying it,' Lisa agreed.

'And to think we nearly killed ourselves climbing out

of the window of the ladies' loo in the restaurant—not to mention ruining my pantyhose,' Angie complained.

'Never mind,' Lisa comforted her. 'I rather think our experiment is going to be a success, after all.'

'That reminds me,' Joy said earnestly. 'The Easter holidays are coming up, and I just *happened* to see a photograph of a really gorgeous film actor. A bachelor, of course. Do you think we could. . .?'

Harlequin Presents...

The beauty of true romance...

The excitement of world travel...

The splendor of first love...

unique love stories for today's woman

Harlequin Presents...
novels of honest,
twentieth-century love,
with characters who
are interesting, vibrant
and alive.

The elegance of love...
The warmth of romance...
The lure of faraway places...

Six new novels, every
month — wherever
paperbacks are sold.